A RICH GIRL'S LOVE

A RICH GIRL'S LOVE

Amber Dana

Chivers Press • G.K. Hall & Co.
Bath, England Thorndike, Maine USA

This Large Print edition is published by Chivers Press, England, and by G.K. Hall & Co., USA.

Published in 2000 in the U.K. by arrangement with Robert Hale Ltd.

Published in 2000 in the U.S. by arrangement with Golden West Literary Agency.

U.K. Hardcover ISBN 0-7540-4013-5 (Chivers Large Print)
U.S. Softcover   ISBN 0-7838-8845-7 (Nightingale Series Edition)

The text of this Large Print edition is unabridged.
Other aspects of the book may vary from the original edition.

Set in 16 pt. New Times Roman.

Printed in Great Britain on acid-free paper.

British Library Cataloguing in Publication Data available

Library of Congress Cataloging-in-Publication Data

Dana, Amber, 1916–
    A rich girl's love / by Dana Amber.
       p.   cm.
    ISBN 0-7838-8845-7 (lg. print : sc : alk. paper)
    1. Children of the rich—Fiction.
    2. Grandfathers—Fiction.   3. Large type books.   I. Title.
PS3566.A34 R53   2000
813'.54—dc21   99-054774

CHAPTER ONE

THE TOLMANS

It was not especially profound, and it certainly had been said before, but like eating, commonplace though it might be, when the need arose it became very significant.

It was significant the day Grandfather Tolman said it, because that was the first anyone knew that Patricia's young man had gone.

'It takes all kinds to make a world, and if a body lives long enough he will meet up with just about every blessed kind there is.'

People heeded Grandfather Tolman because he was hard-headed, shrewd without trying to be clever, but primarily because he it was who made the Tolman fortune. Everything else came afterwards, like higher education for the family, trips abroad, the Tolman Estate, the servants and cars, and the accruals that came as regular as clockwork from the uranium mine in Colorado—source of it all— and from Grandfather Tolman's subsequent investments, gilt-edged each and all.

But otherwise David Tolman, the son, and Elyse the daughter-in-law, would have liked it so much better if Grandfather Tolman had lived somewhere else. Colorado, possibly, or

Timbuktu. He was not always either grammatical nor circumspect in his language. He was blunt enough to make a scoundrel wince, and he had the most uncanny ability of being able to look at a man, listen to him for a moment or two, and define his integrity, honour, and morals in five to ten words.

He was individualistic and always had been. Otherwise, of course, he'd never have gone poking and muttering all over the West looking for 'colour', and eventually finding it, thanks to his Yankee shrewdness. He was also close to seventy-five and Elyse's secret hope that he might quietly lie down and decently disintegrate seemed farther from fruition at age seventy-five than it had at sixty-five.

But Elyse bore her burden with noble fortitude. Her own father, contrary to her little hints, hadn't been one of *the* Morgans. He had been Abe Morgan—née Morganstern—one-time assistant coroner of Cayhauga County, New York. But Elyse was handsome in her late thirties, fair and blue-eyed and with a flawless complexion, so, along with the Tolman wealth, she had no difficulty being accepted anywhere.

Dave, her husband, looked a little like his father. He was a rawboned, wide-shouldered man with brown eyes, curly greying hair which had once been brown also, and he stood slightly over six feet in height. Where he and his father differed basically was that Dave's generation had never worked, and

2

Grandfather Tolman's generation had never done anything but work. The older man was like rawhide and barbed-wire, the younger man had the frame and the constitution, but having been robbed of both need and desire, had never toughened even his hands by manual labour.

Patricia, at twenty-two, was as fair as her mother but with her father's curly hair and lean build. She was long-legged, lithe, and very athletic. She was also a University graduate with a major in education and a minor in pubescent psychology. Grandfather Tolman said he not only had no idea what pubescent psychology was, he couldn't even begin to spell it. He also said, when that suitor dropped from sight, that if pubescent psychology included any decent incantations, why then Patricia ought to get that young man back here, then punch him right square in the nose.

He told Elyse that if she had no objections, he would buy Patricia another young man so she'd stop going about the estate looking like someone in the final throes of lungfever.

Elyse had appealed to her husband, and David went to the wing of the house where his father had rooms, and tried to be subtle, something he never should have tried, and should have *known* not to try, because he'd never been very successful at it with his father throughout all the growing years when he'd been trying subtlety.

'The point is, Father, the less any of us say about Patricia's unfortunate interlude, the better all round. I realize better than anyone your remark to Elyse was with the best of all intentions, but it does appear that Patricia will have to suffer through alone. That's all part of growing up, eh?' Dave winked at his father and richly chuckled.

Grandfather Tolman smiled fiercely. 'Yeah, it's part of growing up, Davey, but I had no idea you knew that.' The fierce smile lingered. 'You never had a heartbreak. In fact, Davey, you never had no suffering of any kind that I recall. Your mother sure wanted the best of everything for you, and by God you got it, son. You got it. As for Pat; don't worry, I'm not going to do anything that'll augment her agony. Although at twenty-two you'd be surprised how fast hearts heal—and skulls too, for the matter of that. Incidentally, Davey, I'd appreciate it if you'd pass words to the servants that I'm expecting a man named MacDonald to come round looking for me today.'

David Tolman's eyes narrowed slightly. 'MacDonald . . . ?'

Grandfather did not take the cue. He simply scowled and said, 'Yas, dammit, MacDonald. Anything wrong with that?'

'No. No, of course not, Father. I was just wondering . . . if perhaps there is some business difficulty . . . ?'

The old man marched to a humidor beside the fireplace, dug for a thick, dark cigar and lit it, then he turned and looked down at his son, who was still sitting. 'Davey, funny thing a father and son can *look* so much alike, without *bein'* alike. God rest your mother, she was a fine woman. I don't blame her, I blame myself for puttin' up with some of her notions. Otherwise maybe we wouldn't be so different. What I'm getting at is simply this: You run the social end of things and I'll run the business end. You got about as much a head for business as I got—for the other part.'

Patricia, polished off very early in this meeting, was brought up once again before her father retreated. He told Grandfather Tolman she had said she thought she'd join one of those overseas youth movements like the Peace Corps and go serve the underprivileged. The old man's reaction was presaged by a cloud of bluish, rank-smelling cigar smoke. Then he said, 'Oh for God's sake, what kind of tommyrot is this? What does Pat know that she can teach people who've been eating ants for ten thousand years? Too bad they did away with the French Foreign Legion. She could have gone off to them and spent four years *really* feeling sorry for herself. Peace Corps indeed! Idealistic tommyrot. You people, Davey, with your exalted sense of superiority turn my stomach. Better it should be the other way around. Let those underprivileged people

5

come and teach you what the real values are, what real poverty and ingenuity and serenity are.'

Grandfather Tolman stamped to the door, opened it and made a gesture as though he were heaving a physical weight from the room. 'Go on now, Davey. And tell Elyse I won't buy Pat another young man.'

The son rose, pained, and went to the door. He paused as though to say something but his father held up his hand, with cigar ash falling to the rug. 'Take Pat up to the lake, Davey. Leave her up there for a few days. If she returns still wanting to go and play Great White Goddess somewhere—good riddance.' The old man closed the door and went over to answer the telephone on his beautiful antique rosewood desk—with the cigar scars on it.

'Tolman here,' he growled. 'MacDonald . . . ? Listen to me; the only person who is ever interested in an excuse, Mister MacDonald, is the man who makes it. Now then—your appointment was to see me here today. I didn't make it any more specific than that as a favour to you. As a damned courtesy. Now you see me here today!'

The old man put down the telephone, squinted at the ash on his cigar, was surprised that it was no longer than it was, then turned and very carefully scrutinized the rug. But he didn't look as far as the door, and it didn't matter anyway. His wife had been dead seventeen years; she was the only person he'd ever known who could draw up to her full height and glare him down. That happened every time he spilled cigar ash, so the feeling of guilt was not dead even yet, after all those years.

He was through with the cigar anyway. He hadn't smoked one through in years. There had been a time when he gently tamped them out and kept the halfsmoked butts in a tin canister, but that too had been many years ago. Now, what he paid for one Sumatra filler was more than he'd paid for a week's supply of stogies forty years before, when he'd been acting like a looney and looking for metals no one else saw any future in.

There was a light knock on his reception-room door. He put the cigar in a huge glass ashtray, got settled in the comfortable leather chair behind his desk, then sang out for whoever it was to enter.

The air was blue with smoke when Patricia Tolman entered, made a face, and without more than a bare nod at her grandfather, crossed to a tall window and flung it open to admit the springtime air and garden fragrance.

'You're going to pollute the whole house,' she told him. 'And you know perfectly well what Doctor Severns said. A man your age shouldn't abuse—'

'That'll damned well be enough,' roared Grandfather Tolman. 'And just how old is

7

Doctor Severns?'

'What's that got to do with it?'

'Plenty! I'm almost eighty. He's about forty. When *he's* eighty I'll listen to him.'

The beautiful girl glared. 'You're just past seventy-five. Grandfather, why do you say that? It sounds awful. And look how old it makes Mother and Dad appear.'

The old man's shrewd eyes measured the girl. She was soft, yet firm, creamy-complexioned, yet tanned and golden. She was, in his view, very delectable, very beautiful. He shook his head. Something like a half century back he'd have risked his happy home just to be able to wink and smile at anything this pretty.

He said, 'Tell me the truth, Pat.'

'You know Mother doesn't like you to call me that.'

'Pat,' he said again, spitting it out. 'Pat—tell me the gospel truth. Why did your young man leave?'

The lovely girl didn't wilt. She didn't even drop her eyes as though his question had opened a fresh wound. She said, 'He wasn't ready for marriage, Grandfather.'

'Oh hell,' snorted the old man. 'He was twenty-five. I've known 'em marry when the lad was eighteen, the girl sixteen. Now listen to me—alibi all you like with your folks and friends, but tarnation, Pat, you be frank and man-to-man with me. After all, at my age I just

8

don't have a lot of time to shilly-shally around the bush. Now straight out: Why?'

She turned, now, and went to stand with her face into the gold sunlight of the opened window. 'He said I was too headstrong, too domineering.'

The old man suddenly smiled so broadly his leathery, lined face threatened to split. 'Well now, that's something, child. That's something. Good for him.'

She turned, cheeks rosy and eyes fiery. 'Good for him . . . ?'

'Sure, Pat. It means *someone* in this house inherited the Tolman spunk!'

CHAPTER TWO

MACDONALD

They called him 'Mac' for an obvious reason although his given name was Joseph. He was six feet tall, about the same height as Grandfather Tolman, or at least as Grandfather Tolman had been at MacDonald's age, but he was thicker, with powerful arms, shoulders and chest.

He had carroty hair, sun-bleached to a rusty dark colour, and tawny eyes set in a square-jawed, rather craggy face. He was a little brusque when he was ushered into

9

Grandfather Tolman's reception-room and the folder he had brought along appeared as a weapon the way he strode over and dropped it on the rosewood desk then stood gazing bleakly at the leathery old man behind the desk.

'I've had time to think over what you said Mister Tolman and—'

'About developing the land?'

'No, not about developing the land, and would you object terribly if I were allowed to finish? What you said about the only person interested in excuses being the man who made them.'

'Sit down, Mister MacDonald.'

'I'll stand. That wasn't an excuse. At least it wasn't an alibi, when I tried to tell you this morning about having to put our meeting off until tomorrow. There was a crew from state realty commission up to see me this afternoon. I didn't know they were coming until an hour before I called you. So you see, it wasn't an excuse, it was business, plain and simple.'

'Sit down—Mister MacDonald!'

'No thanks! And I saw them, then I drove like a maniac to get down here and keep our appointment.'

'*Will* you sit down!'

'No I *won't* sit down! And that folder in front of you is the plans I've completed of the development, plus cost-estimates, plus surveys and bills to be paid. As for the men from the

10

realty commission, they said we were doing everything according to the land development laws of California, so you're in the clear. And—my resignation is on top of all the other papers in the damned folder—*Mister* Tolman!'

Four seconds of silence ensued. MacDonald, oaken in build, and evidently also in temperament, glared. Grandfather Tolman's turkey-track, scraggy neck was red as he rose and crossed to the humidor, bent to select a cigar, then slammed the humidor closed without taking one, and turned to say, 'Mac, if you had explained all that to me . . .'

'What are you talking about, damn it all— Mister Tolman? You hung up the telephone before I had a chance to explain anything!'

'Well, you could have called back.'

MacDonald stood glaring. 'I could have sent a telegram too. Or I could have telephoned a local messenger service. Mister Tolman, I'm past thirty; I stopped playing games the day I left college with an engineering degree. You find someone else to put up with your temperament.'

'*My* temperament. Damn you, MacDonald, you're yelling your head off right now acting like one of those Hollywood movie directors. *My* temperament indeed! Now you listen to me. I only went into that land-development scheme up on the Grapevine because you agreed to ramrod it for me. If you quit now I'll take you to court!'

11

'Go ahead,' said MacDonald, but holding his roar to a window-quivering snarl. 'I'm not going to fight you, I'm going to find another job.'

Grandfather Tolman, mouth open to hurl an imprecation, checked himself and started back for the desk. He even tried to smile, but it was rather ghastly. 'All right, all right.' He sank down into his leather chair, leaned and folded both hands atop the desk while he studied the powerful man before him. 'Would you please sit down? It makes it easier to talk when folks are sitting.'

MacDonald wavered but did not immediately yield. The older man turned to what was now in his mind. 'It's odd, you know, Mac, how sometimes you meet a man who usually says the right thing. Spontaneously; not to ingratiate himself, but just because he thinks right.'

MacDonald looked wary. 'What are you talking about, now?'

'You said you wouldn't fight me in court, that you were only interested in getting back to work. Now that's how a *man* thinks, Mac. But how many real men do you meet nowadays?'

'Just as many as ever,' replied the tawny-eyed younger man, looking round at the chair nearest him, and stepping a little stiffly towards it. 'As for fighting you in court—the reason I said that, Mister Tolman, was because I don't have the time. When I've got as much

12

as you have, maybe I'll go round being obnoxious with law books. As yet, I'm still trying to get up there. And . . . also because you'd never get to first base suing me because we never had a contract.'

Grandfather Tolman's shrewd eyes darkened slightly. But he controlled himself, and that was something because he hadn't had to take back-talk from anyone for forty years. Finally, still pushing that ghastly smile, he said, 'All right, Mac . . . I apologise.' Whether MacDonald knew it or not, those were the two most detestable words in the entire English language to Old Dave Tolman. 'I should have let you have your say over the telephone.'

Grandfather Tolman opened the folder MacDonald had brought, scanned the first, crisp sheet of paper, then lifted it out with two fingers as though it could coil and strike, held it over the basket beside the desk, and dropped it in. Then he waited.

MacDonald crossed thick legs and sat in glum thought for a moment before heaving wide shoulders in a shrug. He could, of course, have capped his triumph with a warning to his employer about the very next time Old Dave cut him off like that, but he didn't. In fact, he didn't utter a sound. The meeting of their eyes was enough, plus the square-jawed set of MacDonald's features.

Grandfather Tolman sighed, as though a storm had just passed without doing any real

13

damage, and began to skim through the other papers in that manila folder.

'How much longer,' he eventually asked, in a totally different tone of voice, 'before we're ready for the sales campaign?'

'A month, maybe. Possibly a little more. But that's based on the assumption nothing will go wrong.'

'What can?'

'Equipment breakdowns, inspection delays from the realty commission, even a big rainstorm.'

The older man fell to examining a map in the folder. 'Water?' he muttered, and when MacDonald said the well-drilling operation was finished, and it had been very successful, he then said, 'Rights-of-way?'

MacDonald's brows dropped. 'Mister Tolman, those were taken care of before we moved in the heavy equipment. You know that.'

Tolman looked up, smiling, but his shrewd eyes seemed to be turning something over in his mind that he hadn't mentioned. He wasn't going to mention it either, obviously, because he rose and shoved out a scarred and bony old hand. 'Thanks for coming, Mac. No hard feelings?'

The younger man rose and gripped the extended hand, dropped it and scanned the leathery old face with a hint of dawning suspicion, but he too, kept back his private thoughts.

'Are you coming up?' he asked. 'I thought you might like to look at things as they now stand.'

Tolman nodded. 'Be up in a few days, Mac. My granddaughter—you've met her haven't you?—she's giving a surprise birthday party for my son. I'll have to hang around for that. Then I'll be up.'

MacDonald nodded, reached for the folder, tucked it under his arm and said, 'I've got a college boy doing the paperwork for me. If I'm not around when you arrive, send him out to find me.'

Grandfather Tolman nodded and saw his guest out. Then he strolled back to the humidor, opened it looking pleased and considered the array of expensive cigars lying so invitingly in their aluminium cartridges, each one individually cased.

He didn't take one. He closed the humidor exactly as he'd done at the height of the recent unpleasantness, and walked out of the reception-room and down a cool corridor with a vaulted ceiling, bound for the rear garden where the tennis court and swimming pool were. Usually, this time of day, and this time of year, his granddaughter was in one or the other of those places. Sometimes alone, but more often with friends. She was a very popular girl. Always had been, except that the boys either treated her with deference or with the kind of comradeship that indicated they recognized her will was as strong as their own and viewed her not as a lovely girl but as an equal.

Grandfather Tolman had noticed that years back, when she'd first gone away to the University, then had brought back a new set of friends. He had never made up his mind which he disliked worst, the fawning, or the coolness.

She was out there, but instead of being in the pool she was reading a book in the shade of an immense old pepper tree, the bane of every gardener they'd ever had because its little red balls poisoned the ground and no grass would grow anywhere close, and also because despite their loudest lamentations the Old Man would not permit the old tree to be cut down and done away with. 'The shade,' he stubbornly argued year in and year out, with the feeling of a man who knew what real tree-shade could mean to a dehydrated man in a treeless country, 'is worth a hundred times more than all the damned green grass that'd grow there, any time.'

The tree stood, shed its berries, and with its spicy scent, looked shaggy and unkempt and raffish no matter how the gardener struggled to give it a proper appearance He went over into its shade, smiled when Patricia looked upwards, and tested the lawn-swing as he always did, even though it had never dumped him, and said, 'For someone about to embark

16

for Peru, you don't act like you're in a hurry to be gone.'

The beautiful face was blank. 'Peru . . ?'

'Your daddy said you were considering joining one of those outfits that send American superiority to the poor and needy Indians—or somewhere.'

Patricia put her book aside and laughed. 'No, not really. It was just a suggestion.'

Grandfather Tolman nodded. 'You wouldn't like it. I'm not saying you couldn't do it, mind. Only that you wouldn't like it. As for the downtrodden . . . Pat, they've always been with us and they always will be. It's noble as all hell to want to help them. But you're not going to change anything that's God-given, and that's resisted change for ten thousand years.'

'Is that any reason not to try, Grandfather?'

He rubbed thin palms together. One of the worst things to arise out of equal opportunities for women was this kind of sharp logic. Fifty years ago a girl would never have said any such thing. Thought it, maybe, but not said it.

'Maybe not,' he conceded. 'But if you succeeded in hoisting these people up, what would they do?'

'Live better, Grandfather, eat better, get an education.'

'Naw. They'd have more children. That's all. And you'd be right back where you started from. Now if you could herd all the young bucks into one big room and—'

17

'Grandfather!'

He studied his freshly rubbed palms a moment, then smiled up at her. 'Anyway, I'm glad that was just a fool notion. I've been thinking about something.' He saw the clear blue eyes harden towards him just a little, the full mouth tighten slightly. He sighed inwardly. That was another bad thing about sending her to the University. She got suspicious of people the moment they wanted to help.

'That land-development up on the Grapevine, Pat, has got to the point where Mister MacDonald just simply can't carry the whole load himself. He's an engineer, not an office clerk. The paperwork's getting too much.'

'I see. You think I could help?'

Grandfather Tolman leaned back in the treacherous swing and beamed. 'Exactly.'

'Grandfather, tell me honestly—am I really needed up there, or is this some scheme of yours to get my mind off my shattered romance?'

'Patricia Tolman, how can you say such a thing to your own grandfather. You ought to know me—'

'That's why I asked you, dear. Because I know you.' She laughed at his expression of outrage. 'Incidentally, how is the sub-division coming?'

'I just told you. MacDonald's being snowed-under with paperwork and visiting officials

18

from the realty commission, and pretty soon now, in about a month or so, we'll be starting work on the promotional aspects. Pat, I really need you up there.' Grandfather Tolman paused, then said, 'The company will pay you the going wage, plus mileage, plus subsistence. And if you get snake-bite, we'll pay hospitalization.'

Patricia's curly hair shook when she laughed, this time. 'Snake-bite? What kind of a sub-division are you involved with?'

'Tell you what; as soon as this confounded party for your dad is over, we'll drive up there. How's that?'

'Fine.'

CHAPTER THREE

FRAIL HUMANITY

There were any number of most excellent reasons for people to live in Southern California. One was that parties could be given any month of the year, with sunshine almost guaranteed.

Whatever the other reasons were, at times it seemed that two-thirds of the entire nation had come to hold them up as a modern ethic, because people had been moving into the State at the rate of a thousand a day for over a decade. If this made land-developers gloat and wax lyrical—as well as rich—it did not always meet with the approval of the natives.

Not that Elyse Tolman ever considered such a thing. She had come from New York twenty years earlier, and after marrying David Tolman had learned to view her environment as an extenuation of the New England social theme. David did too, for although he was a native, his education had been exclusively Eastern—his mother had seen to that—so actually he was a native Californian only because it said so on his birth certificate. In every other way he was an easterner.

For Patricia and her mother to invite the proper people to David's surprise party was simple enough; they merely took the membership list of the Brentwood Country Club and ticked off the names of prominent people they knew and liked. David might have made a different choice, but not widely different, so they sent out the invitations and the day of the party with glittering people arriving pink, laughing and socially correct, Grandfather Tolman, a reluctant part of the conspiracy, took his son off to his own wing of the mansion, ostensibly discussing business with him so his son would not know the house was filling up, until his wife came to get him, thus creating the surprise.

Grandfather Tolman, a lonely man in soul and possibly in heart as well, but never lonely in the brain where it really mattered—self-made men never are—had, over the years, sought a blood-line ethos with his son. He had never quite found it; as soon as Davey said something inane the old man, who was not and never had been notorious for his patience, exploded. As now when Davey remarked, in response to his father's comments about the land development undertaking in the pine-topped mountains that separated Los Angeles from the oil-and-cotton city of Bakersfield, northward, that the family simply did not need money that badly; at least not badly enough so that an old man of seventy-odd should spend his days and nights worrying over it.

'Well, for the love of heaven, Davey, how can you be so damnably blind? What does a man of eighty have left? Can I go chasing girls? If I caught one what would I do about it? And since I detest parties, and flowers unless they grow wild, and haven't read a decent book in twenty years, what am I supposed to do? Go and climb into a tomb and wait? You idiot, Davey; even *old* people have to live for something, and making money is about all that's left!'

'Father, you are *not* eighty,' said Davey firmly.

The old man ran to his humidor, grabbed out a cigar and lit it with cheeks working in bellows-like unison. Then he shook the cigar like a mace in his son's direction.

'Seventy, eighty, ninety, the only difference is you are either alive or dead, that's all. Because most other things have dropped away before you reach seventy. Davey, I hope you go broke someday. No, no, I don't hope that. You're too old to come back. You don't have the bounce anyway. Well, I wish to hell you'd just *sweat* a time or two. Not *perspire*, like Elyse says—just *sweat*.'

'Getting back to the land-development,' said Davey, unperturbed because he was impervious. He'd been undergoing these bombardments since his eighteenth birthday. 'Getting back to that, Patricia told us at dinner last night you offered her a job as secretary to Joseph MacDonald.'

'I see. And Elyse raised hell, and you propped it up for her?'

'We had been talking about sending her east to visit the Morgans in Cayhuaga County.'

This was a real threat and the old man recognized it as such at once. After all, he was the *grand*father not the parent. He slackened his stance and held the cigar so that objectionable smoke would not annoy his son. 'Listen, Davey, for just a minute. I'm up to my gullet in this land deal, and money or not, needed or not, if I lose on this it could seriously hinder the entire family. Now I need someone up there I can trust.'

Davey looked surprised. 'You don't trust Joseph MacDonald? I interviewed him myself,

22

Dad, and his recommendations were absolutely—'

'No, sonny, now I'm not saying we didn't hire the best man at all. The point is, MacDonald is being drowned by paperwork and appointments and engagements, and he's simply got to have a secretary. Now I thought, Patricia being qualified and intelligent, and level-headed, she could keep things orderly.'

'I see. Well . . .'

'Davey, remember son, I'm not as young as I used to be. Why, even five years ago I could have taken all this in stride. I'd have gone up there myself . . . I may still have to do it, although altitude always makes me short of breath and brings on those chest pains . . .'

'No. Don't you go up there,' said Davey, rising and looking slightly contrite. 'Of course Elyse won't object. Anyway, it's only good business, isn't it, having one of the family keeping an eye on things?'

'Exactly son, exactly.'

Providentially, a knock sounded across Grandfather Tolman's reception-room, and when the door opened Elyse was standing there looking radiant and youthful. She even gave Grandfather Tolman an unqualified smile. Of course, there was the width of the room between them.

'Davey,' she said, 'come along now, will you? We have a guest or two.'

Davey nodded and looked back at his

23

father, who was now behind his desk with the cigar smoking from behind his back—Elyse detested the sight as well as the smell of cigars. They smiled affectionately at one another and David Junior left with his wife.

Grandfather Tolman sucked on his cigar and studied the design on the back of the door that had closed behind his son and daughter-in-law.

It was useless. Davey was too old to change, too weak to want to, and too dull to achieve it even if someone made him make the effort.

He heard the music later on, when he went strolling in the north area of the garden, which was directly behind his rooms, and he had the good fortune to discover the neighbour's dog, a fawn-coloured, black-nosed German canine of some breed with pointed ears, sneering through the hedge, and nearly clipped the beast with a well-aimed rock. That helped his mood.

Otherwise though, he had justification for his malaise. In the old days he'd have had five or six schemes going through his head simultaneously. Now, there was just the one: that land development undertaking.

If it netted half as much again as he'd sunk into it he would he satisfied. It couldn't possibly net more and the risk that it might net less, which of course was the equivalent to disaster because of the enormous risk.

'Peanuts,' he growled at the wary dog. 'But

24

that damned Internal Revenue outfit will be there for their capital gains tax the minute I break even and head for a profit. And here I am, an old man, lonely and—'

'Grandfather?'

He turned, ceased his mumbling, and squinted up where Patricia stood on the immense marble gallery connected to the rear of the house. She was dressed in a lovely afternoon cocktail dress with her curly hair shining in sunlight, her breasts high, her shoulders and arms a beautiful shade of tan.

He sighed as he began retracing his steps. 'MacDonald,' he said under his breath, sounding bitter about it, 'you don't deserve it, and maybe someday I'll have to break you because of her, but what's left if I'm going to breed guts back into this tribe of dimpled fops?' Louder, he said, 'Yes, Pat, what is it? And I'm *not* going to get dressed up like a damned penguin just to see your father pronounced one year older.'

'I'm sorry to say, Grandfather, that no one ever thought you'd do that, even for your own son.'

'Then what is it?'

'Well, there is a gentleman in the office from the Revenue Service.' By the 'office' she meant her grandfather's reception-room. Everyone in the house called it his office, which in fact it had always been, furnished as one or not.

25

The old man stopped just short of the long, low steps below the gallery. 'You see, Pat? Starting their hounding already and we haven't turned a red cent in profit yet. I wish I was young enough to go throw him out.'

'Grandfather, he's coming to discuss depreciation schedules for you, on the development. He said you were entitled to more than you'd claimed in the estimate.'

'Why the devil didn't you say that at once? All right, go back to the party.' Grandfather Tolman got up the steps, stopped in the shade and smiled. 'You're the prettiest thing I've seen in fifty years, Pat.'

She leaned and pecked him on the cheek. She smelled of soap and sunshine. 'If you'd prefer I could sit in with the tax-man and you. If I'm to become part of the Tolman establishment, shouldn't I begin about now?'

'Oh hell, child,' muttered the old man, touched more than he'd have admitted under the pain of being beheaded. 'You go on back and keep the party going. And before I forget it, come and see me this evening. I've got something for your father. All right?'

She nodded gently at him. 'I'll come. When do you want to take me up to my new job?'

'Tomorrow? No, tomorrow that damned doctor is due. Day after tomorrow?'

'Fine. What shall I wear?'

That made him blink. 'Wear? Why, whatever women would wear of course. How would I know?'

She went with him as far as the door, then turned off in a different direction. He watched her lithe stride and supple grace, turned and went marching to the meeting with the tax-man.

Grandfather Tolman was not anti-government. He wasn't actually anti-Revenue Service, but he *was*, and regardless of which political party was in office, against *that* party at *that* time.

When he entered the reception-room and found a thin young man standing at the window looking out across the rear grounds, he said, 'Well sir, one of the hopes of my life has been achieved today.'

The young man turned and smiled with respect. 'Yes sir?'

'That nest of anarchists in Washington has finally discovered what every businessman has known for half a century: You can't stifle initiative or the country will go to hell in a hand-basket.' The old man pointed. 'Have a chair!'

'My name is Roger Holloway, Mister Tolman. I explained to your granddaughter why I'm here.'

'Extra depreciation on that wretched disaster that's bankrupting me up in the mountains. Care for a cigar, Mister Holloman?'

'No thank you, sir. Hollo*way*. I've brought

along the estimates submitted by your accounting firm on that land-development enterprise, Mister Tolman. Just to refresh your memory.'

'Glass of sherry, Mister Hillsman?'

'No thank you. It gives me gas.' The young man peered out at Grandfather Tolman as though debating the usefulness of making another pronouncement of his name. Then he sighed and brought forth a thick sheaf of papers. 'The main trouble with these estimates is that we seem always to have to adjust them later.'

'Foolish business, even requiring them. Why can't the confounded government wait until the profit is made—if any—then come steal its share?'

'Yes. Do you mind if I put these papers on your desk, Mister Tolman?'

'No. By all means. I'm an old man and don't see so good any more. And there's my hearing. Pull your chair closer, young feller. I'll have to lean on you for help, you see; as a man gets into his eighties he has some trouble concentrating. Yes, that'll be fine. It's a nice chair, isn't it? I enjoy it myself these cold summer nights. Blood's thin lately. Well now, young man, I'll listen while you explain.'

CHAPTER FOUR

DIFFERING OPINIONS

To reach the development was not difficult. It was rather a matter of selection. There were three passes leading through the coast range of mountains—hills, actually—traversing the countryside from south to north. From Brentwood, where the Tolman estate was, it was simplest to drive east on Sunset Boulevard to Sepulveda Boulevard, thence northward into, and across, the San Fernando Valley, and out of the valley at the town of the same name—San Fernando—and across the miserable desert around Newhall and up that splendid road called the Grapevine, because in olden times it had been that twisty and crooked, although now it was less crooked. In fact, now it was a high-speed expressway although it was still a long climb to the pine-scented, forested top, where the descent began towards the Bakersfield area beyond.

It was near the crest where the only cool, fragrant, clean fresh air for fifty miles in any direction could be found. Also, depressingly hot as summertime Los Angeles became, on top of the Grapevine it was always blessedly cool in the hottest weather. Also, though no one wishing to sell plots of land up there to city-dwellers ever mentioned this, it snowed on the crest. In fact, by midwinter there was snow hip-high to tall Indians up there.

But this wasn't winter. Furthermore, the Grapevine crest had an additional advantage: It was within quick driving time of downtown Los Angeles. Anyone seeking to escape the heat, the smell, the noise and chaos, social and otherwise, of the metropolis, could be on top of the Grapevine in a couple of hours. It had been this, in particular, that had first got Grandfather Tolman interested. He was not a land-developer, but he'd seen fortunes made in the environs of Los Angeles in this field, so when he first heard of the five hundred wooded acres on the crest, he went to look at it. After that, his mind made up, the negotiations began. He ended up owning it, and with a fresh interest, he became brisk and shrewd—and sly as ever.

On the drive up the day after his appointment with the doctor, he told his granddaughter that according to his estimates, based on MacDonald's figures, when he was sold out up there, he should realize not less than a million and a half dollars profit.

She was delighted for him, and also, she hoped nothing would happen to mar his sense of achievement. He smiled. 'That's why I need you up here. Look after our interests.'

There was an office beside a shady road where enormous pine trees stood. Tree-squirrels watched as Grandfather Tolman and his granddaughter got out of the car to stand for a moment stretching and breathing deeply of the delicious air. The squirrels were accustomed to ground-bound, two-legged creatures and after an initial examination of them flicked their tails and departed.

Grandfather Tolman had made what might have appeared as an oversight. He had not telephoned ahead to tell MacDonald he was bringing his granddaughter along to work in the development-office. It wasn't really an oversight, it just appeared to be one.

MacDonald was alone in the office. It was cool in there, and chaotic. Desks, tables, even shelves and chairs, were piled with rolled-up maps of one kind and another. When Grandfather Tolman walked in, with Patricia, MacDonald stood up from behind a cluttered table and offered a greeting even as he moved to empty two chairs of their contents—upon the floor—and arrange them for his guests. It was slightly before noon, and somewhere off through the trees could be heard the deep sounds of giant crawler tractors at work making roads, levelling building sites, clearing brush.

Grandfather Tolman asked where MacDonald's assistant was. Out, he was told, helping to drag chain for the surveyors. 'He's happier doing that anyway,' MacDonald explained, and went to examine the coffee pot

31

to see if there was enough left after his morning council with the straw-bosses, to offer his guests some. There wasn't. He shrugged and returned to the desk. 'Interesting insight into the times,' he stated, 'that college boys nowadays would rather pull chain than work in an office. *Engineering* students, at any rate. When I got out of school I thought pulling chain was the same as wearing one.' MacDonald smiled at Patricia. 'Would you like to see what's being done up here, Miss Tolman? I can get someone to show you around.'

Grandfather Tolman cut in swiftly, 'Maybe later, Mac. Right now I'd like her to see the plot-map and the projection for the finished development. And while she's looking at those, perhaps you and I could step outside a moment.'

MacDonald was perfectly willing, but also a bit puzzled. When he followed the older man out into the pine-scented shade where sounds of those distant machines was louder, he looked less apprehensive than belligerent. Grandfather Tolman recognized that look and smiled as he found an old bench beside a huge pine, and sat down.

'Let the lad stay with the surveyors,' he said, showing the cajoling side of his nature.

'I can't do that,' retorted MacDonald, still standing. 'I told you before, the details are getting a little out of hand.'

32

'Well . . . that's why my granddaughter came up with me today, Mac. She's a brilliant secretary, has a very orderly mind and worlds of tact.'

Joseph MacDonald stood gazing downward without moving or saying a word. A tree-squirrel scolded overhead, and a loud-mouthed bird joined in. The old man's smile lingered.

'It'll sound more—business-like—for a girl secretary to answer the telephone, for instance. And she's hell for work. She'll be better as your right hand than any college boy could ever be. Besides, she'll—'

'So that's it,' broke in MacDonald stonily. 'She didn't just happen to come along for the drive, or to see what we're doing up here.' He paused and gently shook his head at the older man. 'Tell me, Mister Tolman, does she know?'

'Of course. What do you think I am?'

MacDonald judiciously passed that up without a reply. 'Are you aware that Crestline Village is presently practically a barracks for construction workers—all male—and that even it I can get her quartered down there, which isn't very likely, she'll be in a pretty damned rough environment? Mister Tolman—take her back with you and let me suffer along with the college-boy secretary. He may not sound well over the telephone, and maybe he doesn't have a brilliant mind, but right now what I don't need is a beautiful female working around here.'

Grandfather Tolman made a little deprecating gesture, still smiling. 'Mac, as a favour to me . . . she needs to learn there's more to life than Brentwood and parties and books, and silly college boys that look like sheepdogs.'

MacDonald sat, finally, beside the older man on the bench, and with a tough stare, said, 'Mister Tolman—why is it that we can't just function as employer and employee? I'm an engineer. I'm doing a good job for you up here. Costs are below estimates, things are pretty much on schedule.'

'Mac, you're doing a splendid job.'

'How do you know? You haven't been over the place since last spring. I mean, over it yard by yard.'

'Well, you've told me everything is going well. And I have the reports. Now, about Patricia . . .'

'No. Mister Tolman, I can't use her. I don't want her around here. Look, she's extremely attractive and I've got equipment-operators, surveying teams, muckers and timber-fallers— all womanless—doing a splendid job. One good-looking female—and I can just about promise you we're going to start having trouble.'

'Bosh,' exclaimed the old man. 'Mac, she'll be in the office and—'

'That's my point, Mister Tolman. She'll be in the office. Those damned workmen don't come near the office now because when they do I pile more work on them. But I'll have to shovel my way through them when they discover I've got a girl in there.'

'Mac, she *needs* this. I'll tell you a family secret.' Grandfather Tolman edged closer and bent his head. 'She was in love. The boy was about to marry her, then he run off and left her broken-hearted.'

MacDonald showed no sympathy at all. In fact, he showed plain scepticism and Grandfather Tolman recognized the expression, so he took back a fresh breath and tried again.

'She sits around down there, Mac, feeling useless. She's the only grandchild I have, and I'll tell you very frankly that if *she* doesn't develop into something, I've accomplished nothing in my seventy-four years. Now, that's the way it is.'

MacDonald still was unmoved. 'Mister Tolman,' he said, enunciating very distinctly and assuming a look of strong patience, 'I'm not a baby-sitter, I'm a construction engineer. You own several factories. Put her in one of them. Maybe you could even use her at home in your office. But up here—it just wouldn't work.' MacDonald rose from the bench as a man in soiled boots and trousers approached. He said, 'What is it, Clem?' The other man smiled at Mister Tolman, then said, 'Broke a friction on one of the D-8 cats, Mac. Got to telephone down to Bakersfield for parts to be sent up. Nothing very terrible.' He veered off and went heading obliquely towards the log-walled office, with MacDonald looking after him.

Grandfather Tolman started to speak, but Mac held out a hand for silence. Then he said, 'Now watch, Mister Tolman. Just sit there and watch.'

Moments later when the equipment-operator strode out of the office he stopped in tree-shade to comb his hair, to slap at dirt on his trousers, and to hitch at his belt. Then, without a glance in the direction of the watching men near the old bench, he struck out rapidly through the forest.

Mac flapped his arms. 'Satisfied?' He looked at his wrist. 'Lunch-break in half an hour, Mister Tolman. The men take their lunch out to the job with them. If you'll hang about you'll see every last one of them come back here to sit around eating. That man will pass the word about the girl in the office. That'll be the beginning of it.'

Mac stood looking down, a deep furrow across his forehead. Grandfather Tolman, sitting in an attitude of close attention, did not look either worried or contrite. He almost looked pleased, although he obviously was not prepared for Joseph MacDonald to see this.

36

'Do the job a favour, Mister Tolman. Take your granddaughter down to lodge in the village, buy her lunch, then head back home with her.'

The older man continued to sit gazing across towards the shady porch that surrounded the log-walled office. After a time he said, 'Well, Mac, I'm disappointed. I figured you was the kind of feller who'd help out a friend.'

MacDonald did not unbend. 'If it were anything but *this*, I'd at least make the effort, Mister Tolman. Look at it from my viewpoint.'

'Yes,' exclaimed the old man, making a great effort of struggling up on to his suddenly rickety, old legs, then leaning heavily against the tree behind the bench.

'Yes, you're probably right. Only there's one more thing. Between the pair of us, Mac, I don't give a damn about the development. Well, of course I *care* about it, but what good's the profit if I've got no one worthwhile to leave it all too? After all, Mac, a man in his eighties don't have too much time left.'

MacDonald fidgeted, but his gaze was unrelenting.

'I honestly wish I could help, Mister Tolman, and if it was anything but *this*. I've got a rough job to do, and I'm doing it, but as you certainly can understand, I can't go *looking* for trouble, can I?'

'I suppose not. Well she'll be crushed, Mac.

37

All she talked about on the drive up here was how wonderful it was going to be, having a chance to be genuinely *useful*. You know, that's very important to people. Especially girls, Mac. They need to feel that they're contributing.'

'I'm sure of it, Mister Tolman, but what she'd be contributing to up here, the only really pretty woman anywhere around, wouldn't be what she'd have in mind. Well, unless you have something else that needs discussing out here, suppose we go back inside. I've got a lot of work to do.'

CHAPTER FIVE

TRAPPED

Only a few years before, Crestline Village had been little more than a clutch of A-frame summer cabins, a curio shop, a petrol station, all clinging to the side of the road. Now, there was a four-storey log lodge, sumptuously furnished in rustic style, plus several motor lodges, grocery markets of respectable size, and a number of other business establishments, including a lumber yard and a quite professional-looking medical clinic.

The Tolman name was known throughout this entire area because of the large development it was connected with. Cheques to most of the building-trades stores in the area with the name 'Tolman' on them, had already established the fact that Tolman wealth, and promptness in paying, was above reproach.

But only a very few people knew Grandfather Tolman by sight, and none knew his granddaughter at all, so when they stopped at the beautiful big lodge for luncheon, although they were treated with respect, there was no deference until after they had eaten, and during that time neither thought of it anyway, because, as Patricia said when her grandfather outlined his plan, 'There is no reason under the sun for you to have put up with that, Grandfather. Mister MacDonald is an employee and nothing else.'

'Well, not quite, Pat. You see—'

'And furthermore, from the condition that office was in before I started setting it to rights, believe me, he definitely needs someone. If the job has been progressing smoothly it's a wonder: You can't even find a *pencil* without moving a ton of drawings and letters and books and whatnot!'

'He's a very stubborn man, child.'

She arched heavy brows. 'Aren't you, Grandfather? I've heard it said that you never took no for an answer.'

'Oh,' smiled Grandfather Tolman, as their food arrived. 'I haven't taken no for his answer, child.' He examined the light salad. He was not a heavy eater. Rather absently he reached inside his jacket, drew forth a wallet, extracted some large notes and put them over in front of Patricia. 'That's to pay your keep here at the lodge.'

She looked dumbfounded. The money was far in excess of what anyone would need for this stated purpose. More uniquely, she had no intention of remaining behind when he went back to Brentwood, and had no idea this was in his mind.

'You see,' he explained, 'Mac is going to hire you. In fact, you're already hired. I'm head of things and I've already taken care of that. But we're going to have to prove to him we Tolmans don't take no for an answer, aren't we? Then there's our private interest, eh? And as you said, yourself, the man needs a qualified secretary.'

'He refused.'

'Bosh! You will have rooms here. Each morning you will go out there and go to work.'

'Grandfather, if he won't let me . . .'

'What do you mean—won't let you? Pat, you *make* him let you. You're my granddaughter and confidant. Don't look so worried—he'll take you in, I promise it.'

Grandfather Tolman beckoned to a waiter and asked if the manager could be brought to their luncheon table.

'I'm David Tolman,' he said. 'This is my

granddaughter, Miss Patricia Tolman.'

The waiter was sure the manager would come and went at once to fetch him. That, finally, was when the deference occurred, but after hearing Grandfather Tolman's request— that a suite be prepared for his granddaughter— the deference was strained a little, for as Joe MacDonald had predicted, the lodge was literally overrun with construction workers.

The old man listened respectfully, then asked for the telephone number, and the name, of the President of the Board of Directors of the company that owned the Crestline Lodge, in his most pleasant tone of voice.

Quarters were found. It was not the suite Grandfather Tolman had requested, but it was a sitting-room with a lovely little private balcony, a spacious, well-furnished bedroom with a bath adjoining, on the second floor where, the manager said, there was a wonderful breeze every afternoon and evening.

The rent was exorbitant but Grandfather Tolman paid it without a murmur. Then he and Patricia went up there to sit briefly on her private gallery, where the old man lit a cigar and relaxed while gazing out over the seemingly endless lift and fall of mountain ridges, all darkened and bristly with forest covering.

He said nothing more about the lodge or

her accomodation. This interlude had only been a minor point anyway. But he *did* suggest that she telephone him, keep him apprised of events.

Her personal reaction was full of doubt. She even accused her grandfather of deliberately manoeuvring her into this unpleasant situation, when he should have simply telephoned MacDonald, laid down the law, then introduced her this morning as MacDonald's new secretary.

He did not argue the issue. He couldn't have because placing her in the secretarial job wasn't really his design. If he'd mentioned what that design actually was, she'd have hit the ceiling. He smiled at her and winked.

'Pat, you've never had to really fight for something before. Well . . . if you fail I'll understand. After all, you're a female.' He made it sound terrible. 'As for laying down the law—child, you've got to learn about men like MacDonald. No one lays down the law to them. He'll walk off.'

'You can replace him,' she said, beginning to sound more disgusted than angry.

'No I can't, Pat. He's started the development from scratch. He's slept with it and lived with it day to day. Even if I brought in another good man, we'd lose a lot of time. The idea is to finish the improvements before winter, so we can start the selling campaign, otherwise we'll lose valuable time. Now listen to me, honey—you're as valuable to this development as he is. But in a different way. You keep him free of details.'

'If he won't let me?'

'He'll let you. You'll see to that. After all, you're my grandchild, aren't you? We don't take no for an answer, do we?'

'Not even if we have to be underhanded about it, Grandfather?'

'Ah now, Pat, you know how it is with old folks. We can't push a fist into someone's face no more, so we got to use our wits. And then there's the—'

'Grandfather, you're an unmitigated fraud. Are you aware of that? You never do anything straight out, it's always got to be sly.'

'But I just explained, Pat. We older folks got to—'

'Older folks indeed! I saw you through the window of the office this morning, when you were so weak and unsteady as you rose off that bench. The way you leaned on the tree slump-shouldered and pathetic. Grandfather, you ought to be ashamed of yourself.'

'I am, child, I am. But you got to understand that high elevation gives me chest pains. Might be the makings of heart trouble or something.'

Patricia rose and went to lean upon the balcony railing for a moment, her face angry, her body slightly stiff. Then she turned on him. 'All right. You've got me into this mess and I can't very well just run out on it. But I'm going to explain to Mister MacDonald exactly what you've done.'

The old man rose and knocked ash from his cigar, smiling gently as though to himself. 'All right, honey. If that'll make you feel better.' The shrewd old eyes lifted slowly. 'Just remember—your job here is not to get him so mad he'll quit, it's to make the job easier for him.'

She said, 'I ought to have my head examined.'

He made a little wheezing sound and leaned to put the cigar into an ashtray on a small table near at hand.

'I guess I'd better be heading on back now. Expect Doc Severns was right yesterday, when he told me I smoked too many cigars. They harden up a man's arteries and all.'

As he turned to go back inside his granddaughter said, 'You are incorrigible.' But she went ahead and held the door for him, and when they were out in the cool, sunlighted hallway she said, 'Why don't you let me drive you back, then I'll return?'

His chest pains vanished. 'Oh no, that's not necessary at all. As soon as I get rolling I'll be just fine.' He reached out and patted her cheek. 'You will do the right thing, won't you, Pat?'

She hooked her arm through his and started down the hallway to the stairs with him. 'I'll do what I can,' she said cautiously. 'But don't be surprised if you get a telephone call tomorrow to come and get me because he wouldn't let me in the office.'

'You can handle him, Pat. I've got all the confidence in the world in you. Of all my kin, I've got the most confidence in you, child.'

The manager was downstairs and came forward to ask if the rooms were acceptable. Grandfather Tolman smiled his nicest little-old-man smile. 'Perfect,' he said. 'Aren't they, child?'

Patricia nodded, then she said, 'Where are the stores? If I'm going to stay on I'll have to buy a few things.'

She cast a reproving glance at her grandfather, which he managed not to see, while the manager explained about Crestline Village shopping facilities, and topped it off by offering to lend Patricia his personal car if she'd care to drive to Bakersfield, which was a large city, for additional shopping.

Grandfather Tolman dug out his wallet, extracted a hundred-dollar note and handed it to the manager with a request he look after Miss Tolman. The manager gave assurances that he would look after her like he'd look after his own daughter.

Outside, with shadows beginning to form although it was early afternoon, Patricia saw her grandfather to his car. She asked when he'd be returning.

'Within a few days,' he assured her, and with

no such intention at all. 'If you'll let me know what I should bring you from home . . .' He reached out and patted her hand. 'Now we're a team, child, eh? The Tolman team. You know, I've always wanted it to be like that.'

At least this statement was pure fact and Patricia knew it. Not that either she or her grandfather despaired of his son and her father, but they both knew, without ever mentioning it, that David Tolman Junior simply was not like Grandfather Tolman, and therefore no partnership would ever ensue.

She smiled, finally, and bent to kiss his cheek. 'But I'd have liked it so much better if you'd handled it another way, Grandfather. This way, you've left it all up to me.'

'Well sure, child. That's the way things should be. You want to meet the world face to face, don't you? No one smoothed the way for me.' Grandfather Tolman paused, then came as close as he'd ever come to revealing his private thoughts about his own son. 'Making things easy for folks, Pat, just isn't the way. It's ruined more men than it's ever made. Believe me, it has.'

She nodded, understanding perfectly, then stepped back so he could drive off. Afterwards, she strolled back towards the huge, delightful verandah of the lodge and stood looking down the road, in the direction her grandfather had disappeared.

It was no trouble at all, being annoyed,

irritated, even disgusted with Grandfather Tolman, but the glimpses she had of what lay beneath the surface, now and then, always kept her off-balance with him. There was no question at all in her mind that she'd been used, this time, as she'd been used other times by him, but there was also just enough understanding to make her feel wistful for him.

And of course that was the whole idea.

She knew that too. The dilemma was, of course, how to combat him. Every time, as at luncheon, when she'd made up her mind to be inflexible, she thought of all the heartbreaks her father had been to Grandfather Tolman over the years, and the inflexibility flexed.

She turned and went through the huge lobby to the stair-well, and went upstairs to have a cool shower, perhaps a nap, then, later on, maybe she'd do a little shopping, get acquainted with the village, and after that, over dinner, she'd start planning how she was going to overcome Joseph MacDonald.

She had no illusions about MacDonald at all. She was not as adept at reading men as her grandfather was, but then he'd been at it a good bit longer. But she had, nonetheless, inherited much of the old man's shrewdness, much of his wiliness too whether she'd have admitted it or not. There was, therefore, a fairly good chance that she might succeed.

CHAPTER SIX

A CLASH OF TEMPERS

Her opportunity came considerably in advance of any warning she had. Joseph MacDonald also lived at the lodge. When he drove in from the development that evening he was not in a good frame of mind. Then the manager, who knew and liked him, sidled up and said, 'I've heard of superintendents being spied on, Mac, but never quite like this. She is beautiful.'

MacDonald scowled. 'Who is beautiful, Frank?'

'The old man's granddaughter.'

'Oh. You saw them at lunch. Well, yes, she is pretty.'

'Her rooms are on the same floor as yours, Mac. But farther down the hall. I managed to get her one of those doubles with the view and the balcony.'

MacDonald stood staring. 'Here?' he said. 'Now?'

The manager nodded. 'The old man went on. She's paid-up for two weeks.'

'I don't believe it.'

'Well, come look at the register. She signed it.'

'He wouldn't do that.'

'He wouldn't?'

'Which suite, Frank?'

'Four-ten on the second floor. Mac, I wouldn't go up if you're feeling angry. After all, she's a lady and the old man is—'

'I know what the old man is,' exclaimed MacDonald, twisting to head directly for the stairs. 'I know exactly what the old man is!'

MacDonald reached the second-floor landing by taking two stairs at a time. He marched down the corridor and thumped Suite Four-Ten's door with a hard fist, and when someone called out, sounding annoyed, asking who it was, he said, 'Joseph MacDonald.'

The answer was not what he expected. 'Go away, Mister MacDonald.'

He was stopped in his tracks. He had expected denunciation, anger, even perhaps a tearfully contrite girl quaking in her boots before the wrath of Joe MacDonald. What he got was some kind of stiff-lipped annoyance, and an order to go away. He struck the door again.

'Miss Tolman, what I want from you is very simple and I can explain it through a door in very few words. Today, while your grandfather and I were outside, and you were tidying things up inside the development office—what the hell did you do with that large yellow sheet of paper that showed when the realty commission people made their work-progress inspections?'

She came to the door, opened it halfway and looked up at him. 'You have a filing cabinet, Mister MacDonald, and that particular form was filed, first, under Inspection, and secondly, under its sub-heading—work-progress.' She did not smile nor raise her voice. 'Now will you go away, so I can get some rest. It's been a long, and very disappointing day, Mister MacDonald.'

'Gladly,' he said, but did not move. 'Would it be asking too much, Miss Tolman, if I enquired why you are here?'

'I work here, Mister MacDonald.'

'Here? In the lodge?'

'No. I *live* at the lodge and *work* at the development office.'

'Oh no, you don't.'

She sighed, leaned on the door a moment, then opened it wider. 'Come in, Mister MacDonald. Since you won't go away, and because hallways are poor places for discussions, please come in where we can at least argue in private.'

He did not move. 'You don't work at the development office, Miss Tolman. I made that clear to your grandfather.'

A vein in the side of her neck swelled. 'Mister MacDonald, you don't make things clear to my grandfather. It's the other way round.' She stepped forward, grabbed his sleeve and pulled. He took two forward steps. She closed the door behind him and turned to

50

cross the sittingroom to the balcony doorway. From over there she said, 'Will you give me just one good reason why I shouldn't work in the development office, Mister MacDonald?'

'I can give you a dozen,' he replied. 'The first one is that you are a pretty girl. I have only men working on the development. Most of them are single, but even the married ones haven't had much chance to get home lately. The last thing I want is a girl in the office. Does that make sense to you?'

She looked at him. 'If that's the best objection you can come up with, believe me Mister MacDonald, I can handle it.'

He threw up his arms and rolled his eyes. 'You can handle it. Young lady, these are not college boys. They are construction *men.*'

She suddenly looked angry. Not at what he'd said, but at the condescending way he'd said it. 'I said I can handle it, Mister MacDonald.' She stepped away from the balcony doorway to face squarely up to him. 'I'm trying not to lose my temper with you, Mister MacDonald, and believe me, I'll be at the office in the morning. But what is it, specifically and individually, that you don't like about me? Don't tell me it's because you think I'll disrupt your labour force because I don't believe that. There is something else. Something private and personal.'

'Private,' he said. 'Personal. What the hell are you talking about? I scarcely know you at

51

all. I've met you two or three times at the Brentwood estate. Until right now we've hardly even spoken. How could I have a personal dislike of you?'

'That's what I'd like to find out.' She looked a little helpless. 'I can't imagine what I've said or done. Unless it's some flaw in you. Perhaps you don't like girls. Something like that.'

She was beginning to make him sound a bit odd and he didn't like that, obviously, for he said, 'Look, it's nothing personal—yet. But if you're as underhanded as that old grandfather of yours, I'll—'

'I won't listen to that kind of talk about my grandfather, and if you had one shred of loyalty in you for the people who pay your salary, you wouldn't even *think* like that.'

MacDonald let all that breath out, took down a fresh one and started over. 'It's nothing personal between you and me, Miss Tolman. But if you are part of your grandfather's conspiracy to goad me into quitting, just come right out and say so. I can save both of us a good bit of time and unpleasantness by resigning right now, tonight.'

She looked at the floor, then over at a chair near the far wall and went towards it to be seated. It was a play for time, obviously, although Joseph MacDonald was probably too irate to realize it.

Her grandfather's admonition was

uppermost in mind. She was not to allow MacDonald to quit, whatever else occurred. She sat down, crossed her legs and looked up at him with a deliberately calm expression. 'Is there any possibility at all of us settling this amicably, Mister MacDonald?'

'It is settled, Miss Tolman.'

'I see. Do you know how it sounds to hear a grown man threaten to quit if everything isn't done his way? When I was a child I had one particular cousin who was so spoilt rotten that if we other children—'

Joseph MacDonald held up a hand. 'I'm paid to work eight to ten hours daily. Not twelve or fifteen. I've been on the job since five this morning and if you'll excuse the expression, I'm pooped. Maybe another time you can tell me about your cousin.' He turned and went to the door. She probably should have risen, if for no other reason than to see him out. She should perhaps have had the last word too. When he turned to nod back, she still said nothing. Then he was gone, the echoing rattle of the closed door filled her rooms, and she said, 'Damn. I don't think I've ever met a more pig-headed man.' She glanced at her wrist. It was time for dinner. She wasn't very hungry but a cup of coffee would taste good.

She rose and went to look at herself in the bedroom mirror before going down through the lounge to the dining-room. She was not entirely unprepared for what she would encounter down there.

What *did* surprise her, however, was the numbers of them. The dining-room held almost nothing but men, all scrubbed but all obviously construction, or heavy-equipment, operators. Burly, youngish, bold men. The moment she stepped through the dining-room doorway raucous conversation dwindled to a whisper. She allowed a waiter to guide her through the forest of yeasty eyes to a table near a large glass door leading out into a rear garden. She wondered if perhaps the waiter had given her this strategic position in case she had to run for it.

Midway through her meal a shiny-faced man with wetted down curly brown hair came to the table and grinned at her. He was somehow familiar to her.

'We met at the office,' he said. 'I'm the guy who used the 'phone this morning. You remember; I ordered a kit for the friction-drive on a D-8 cat.'

'Oh, yes,' she murmured, remembering the man now, but that last sentence went over her head as though each word had been Arabic.

'I didn't catch your name this morning, miss. Some of the fellows were wondering. Are you going to work in the office, out there?'

'I don't know,' she replied. 'I rather doubt it. Mister MacDonald doesn't approve.'

The cat-skinner's brows shot straight up. 'Of

you?'

'Of me—or perhaps just of women working in land development offices.'

'He's out of his tree. You're exactly what's needed out there, Miss . . . ?'

'Patricia Tolman.'

'. . . ? Tolman?'

She smiled. 'My grandfather is David Tolman Senior.'

The curly-headed man's boldness wilted slightly. 'Well,' he conceded, after some thought, 'that *does* make a difference. After all, it's not like some secretary just come up here to work for the company.'

She kept smiling. 'I don't see it that way, Mister . . . ?

'Pete Hudson.'

'Mister Hudson. I have no designs on Mister MacDonald's job and I'm not going to file secret reports about him, about the job, every night. But if you've ever tried to find anything in that office, then you surely know what a hopeless mess it is.'

Peter Hudson nodded. 'I expect so,' he murmured, and bobbed his head, anxious to return to his own table and friends to spread the news about that beautiful, leggy girl. 'Well, good luck anyway,' he said, and hastened away.

Patricia finished her light dinner, had a second cup of coffee, then signed the tab and instead of walking back through that forest of

55

masculine eyes, opened the glass door and disappeared beyond, out into the twilight of the empty garden.

A man's voice said, 'No, not again,' and Joe MacDonald stepped out of her path, where he'd been standing, smoking a crooked-shank little briar pipe.

She stopped, ignored his rudeness and looked up where a mottled old moon, half-full and dim-lighted, rode an empty sky. 'The nights up here are lovely, aren't they, Mister MacDonald?'

He pulled on the little pipe, emitted smoke, looked suspiciously at her, then cautiously nodded. 'Very lovely, Miss Tolman.'

'Mister Pete Hudson thinks it's a shame that you don't want me at the office.'

'Does he now. And you made me look as black as possible, no doubt.'

'I didn't have to. When I told him my name he lost all his boldness. He even thought you were probably right.' She dropped her eyes to his face. 'I think this is the first time in my life I haven't a single friend anywhere around.'

He puffed a moment, studied her, then removed the pipe. 'I detect something of your grandfather in you, Miss Tolman. The tactic of reverting to wile when you can't win another way.'

Her colour came up swiftly. She did not like wiliness in her grandfather; she doubly did not like it in herself, but most of all, since it was possible that she *had* inherited the propensity, she very much resented having this pipe-puffing, rusty-haired bigot accuse her of it.

She threw a round-house blow that connected with Joe MacDonald's cheek with the sound of a pistol shot. He lost his pipe and his head whipped sideways as though it were attached to a rubber neck. She had taken him completely by surprise.

She had also taken herself by surprise. She had never slapped a man before. Under different circumstances she'd been able to discourage them with a look, or a few words.

She flung about and nearly ran back towards the rear of the lodge, where a wide doorway led into the ground floor lounge, near the stairway.

CHAPTER SEVEN

THE NEW DAY

'I'm telling you,' exclaimed Pete Hudson, 'she took him a belt in the chops that'd have downed a horse. I wasn't close enough to hear what he said to her, but it must've sure been the wrong thing. There I was, standing in the shadows of the back porch, and seen them come together out there, and right away I said to myself, this ain't accidental. She'd went and met him out there in the dark. Then—pow! She let him have a right hand that sounded like it was made of cast-iron. Then she run into the lodge and he stood out there looking in the grass for his blasted pipe.'

The listening men hunkered at the bar across the road from Crestline Lodge, where most of the development crew went every evening after dinner for a few beers, because there was nowhere else for them to go, unless it was to bed, and nothing else for them to do after supper.

A man with coarse, Slavic features and small grey eyes looked up at Hudson. 'Couldn't you even hear a word or two of what he said?'

'No. Her back was towards me, sort of. I could see his face, but I couldn't hear him talking.'

'Maybe he didn't say anything at all,' suggested another man.

The Slavic-looking man grunted. 'That don't make sense. She'd never had just walked up to him and swung. Girls don't act like that, you numbskull.'

'No? Then why *did* she swing?'

'You can guess the answer to that as well as I can. Because that damned Joe MacDonald said something dirty right out to her.'

Even Pete Hudson sat perfectly silent after that, and up until now this had all been his show. A tall, fair man near the far curving of

58

the bar shook his head. 'I don't think that. Mac's not the type.'

The Slavic-looking man's little grey eyes got narrower. 'How do you know what type Mac is, Otto? Listen, you don't even know how *I'd* act around a pretty girl right now, let alone—'

'Oh yes I do,' broke in Otto, 'you bet your damned boots I know.'

Everyone but the Slavic-looking man broke out into laughter. Several of the men pushed aside empty beer glasses and got to their feet. It wasn't actually late, but dawn came early at this time of year and people who used backs and shoulders, legs and arms all day long, needed rest.

Gradually, they all trooped back across the road towards the lodge. It was nearly ten o'clock. Most of the upper-storey lights were already out.

Another element seldom encountered at lower elevation was the sweet, tangy night-air. A person's head rarely more than touched a pillow and they slept. For the labour crewmen as with every other inhabitant of Crestline Lodge, this particular night was just like every other. By eleven o'clock the great log building was nearly totally dark upstairs and down.

When dawn arrived it brought a pink light with it. It also brought birdsong and the excited chittering of tree-squirrels. By the time the men trooped into the dining-room to be fed their first meal of the day—they bought

59

pre-prepared box lunches to take with them for the noon meal—Joseph MacDonald had already breakfasted and gone on.

At first, the men made a wry joke out of that, saying MacDonald only did that to make a good impression on the Tolman interests. But since no Tolman appeared on the job except at rare intervals, but otherwise everything always seemed to have been prepared for and anticipated, now the men didn't notice MacDonald's absence.

As for MacDonald, he was never very concerned with the private opinion others seemed to have of him. He was, on the other hand, quite concerned with the opinion he had of himself. He worked hard and took pride both in that fact, and in the gratifying results that followed as a result of hard work.

Also, Mac loved the early mornings. He had driven out to the development office several times and found deer beside the road, or he'd caught the first-dew scent of pine and sumac and chaparral. He thought that first pink light, seen as it filtered through from the overhead heights of the stiff-topped trees, was as beautiful as any light shining through the stained-glass window of a cathedral.

It was less a matter of being a nature-lover than it was being conscious of his oneness with the natural world. MacDonald had been farm-raised, and that made a difference. He never drove *to* the office at sun-up, he instead drove *with* the sun-up to his office.

Only this morning he was the second to arrive, not the first. Patricia had a light on in the rearmost room and Mac, last one out the night before, thinking he'd neglected to turn that light off, went on through, opened the door and blinked.

Patricia had fresh file holders alphabetically arranged on a table from which she took them one at a time and placed them properly in a drawer. She didn't smile when Mac loomed in the doorway, but she said, 'Good morning,' then lifted another folder, turned her back on him, and put the folder in its correct place in the drawer.

He stepped inside, eased the door closed and leaned upon it. 'How did you get in here?'

She turned, still unsmiling. 'The rear door was unlocked.'

He said nothing about that. 'Why are you doing this? You know perfectly well I don't want you here.' Gradually, the artery in his temple began ominously to throb and swell.

She watched the anger rise in him, and said, 'Mister MacDonald—please—-will you just give me a chance? I'm not spying for my grandfather, I'm not after your job, I'm only asking—begging, if you like that better—for an opportunity to do something worthwhile. If you wish, I'll stay out of sight of the workmen.'

He let off a big, pent-up breath. 'Oh Lord,' he exclaimed. 'This is the most ridiculous situation I've ever heard of.' He turned very suddenly, slammed the door behind himself and went into his private, front office, where he grabbed up the telephone and dialled the Tolman estate down in Brentwood. When a servant answered in something like a whisper, MacDonald said loudly, 'Let me speak to Mister Tolman Senior, please.'

The servant's sepulchral tone was full of reproach.

'I'm sorry, sir, but the household is not up yet. If you'll leave your number, Mister Tolman Senior can call you back.'

MacDonald almost retorted. Instead, he put down the telephone, and rose from behind the desk when a man's bull-bass roar from out front caught his attention. He would have to get hold of Old Man Tolman later, right now the work-day was beginning. He strode out into the foremost room of the log-building where a caustic-eyed straw-boss leaning across a map of the entire project gave him a dour look, and said, 'One yell used to bring you. Now it takes three.' The straw-boss pointed with a stubby finger at the map. 'We need more culvert to lay for that second creek under the new road up in the lakeside sub-division area. We got maybe enough to keep the crew working until this afternoon. But first thing in the morning, we'll have to have more.' The straw-boss looked cross. 'How come you don't stock-pile more culvert anyway, Mac? On a job as big as this one it don't pay to skimp.'

MacDonald looked hard at the man. He'd been working with this straw-boss right from the inception, and they'd laughed off much more difficult things than culvert pipe. But he could feel the change in the straw-boss. At a loss to explain it, he simply said, 'Okay, I'll get it up here. Anything else?'

'Nothing,' said the straw-boss, let his gaze wander a bit, looking through the doorway behind MacDonald, then he turned and stalked out of the office.

MacDonald leaned on the nearest map-counter and groaned. So *that* was it. The girl. Exactly as he'd predicted. Somewhere a telephone jangled, harbinger of the fresh new day and the everlasting details that could, insignificant though most proved to be, distract him from what was important. He straightened up off the map-table and went on through to his private office.

The telephone was no longer ringing. MacDonald was not aware, until he walked in and saw her leaning down making a note of something on a large, lined tablet on his cluttered desk, that this was so. Her shoulders, the way she was leaning, showed tanned flesh. The curly hair, worn short—which he'd have approved of, if he'd approved of anything about her—shone with dark, coppery overtones from sunlight through a nearby window.

She said, 'Thank you for calling,' put aside the telephone and, somehow knowing he was standing by the door although she hadn't looked up, she said, 'That was the shipping department of Morris Steel Fabricators down in Los Angeles. They will have the culvert pipe loaded and rolling within the hour.'

He looked steadily at her. 'What culvert pipe are you talking about?'

'The pipe that man just told you about in the front office, Mister MacDonald. I overheard him telling you it was critical. So I telephoned down there.'

'Why Morris Steel, Miss Tolman?'

'Sir, the list of pipe used, and the suppliers, are in our file. It only took a moment to look it up. And another moment to make the call.'

'What *size* culvert pipe, Miss Tolman?'

Her blue eyes wavered. 'Uh—I used one of the transceivers, Mister MacDonald. I asked one of the men working on culvert in the lakeside area.'

Mac stood like a statue. 'Just like that.'

'Wasn't it one of those details that interfere with your regular work?' she asked.

He started a sharp rejoinder, but again the telephone rang. This time, distant though he was, he proved that an adequately motivated man, though large and thick, can move with surprising speed. He beat her hand to the telephone by inches, hoisted the instrument and barked his name. The voice that came back was cool, properly modulated, and incisive. It belonged to Davey Tolman.

'I just heard that you called earlier, Mister MacDonald, and because there might have been something requiring a decision I'm calling back. What is it?'

'I'd like to speak to Mister Tolman, *Senior*,' said MacDonald. 'If he's available.'

'Mister MacDonald, my father apparently suffered a mild heart attack last night. Doctor Severns and my wife are with him. I'm afraid for the time being he won't he able to take any calls. You'll have to settle for me. And incidentally—please don't tell any of this to my daughter. No point in it, her grandfather says. He doesn't want her worrying when she is supposed to be working. Now then, Mister MacDonald . . . ?'

'Well, it's really nothing, Mister Tolman. I . . . was just wondering when he'll be up again, is all. Not for any special reason. Sorry I called so early. Goodbye.'

MacDonald eased the telephone down gently and kept his gaze on it despite his full knowledge that he was being stared at from a distance of no more than six or eight feet. Finally he said, 'Well, you ordered the culvert,' and looked up. 'All right; it was a detail, and you took care of it. What do you expect, the Medal of Honour?'

She stepped around the desk and walked over to the door, opened it and passed through, then soundlessly closed it leaving MacDonald in thought.

He sank down behind the desk. What would happen if the old man died? A mild heart attack could presage a not-so-mild one. He felt like throwing something. At his initial meeting with the Tolmans, junior and senior, he'd been struck by two things: the age of Tolman Senior, and the soft futility of Tolman Junior. But he had only speculated briefly on Tolman Senior's age, for although it was considerable, was in fact even a bit beyond the age of the oldsters one saw in city parks across the land playing draughts or dozing in sunlight, or arguing politics with other oldsters, it had not appeared to MacDonald to be immediately terminal. Now, he was much less sure.

He was reaching for his pipe when the telephone rang again. With both hands occupied he glared and let the instrument ring. Then, as he was free to pick it up, the ringing stopped. He regarded it a moment in mild surprise, then picked it up, clapped it to his ear, and heard Patricia Tolman's voice say: 'I'll take the message for Mister MacDonald, and when he has the time he may return your call. And thank you.'

She hung up. Whoever had called hung up. MacDonald slowly lowered the telephone, which was making its unpleasant humming sound, and he was the last to put his telephone aside.

He resumed loading his pipe. He lit it, puffed a moment to be sure the fire had taken hold, then he gently dropped the dead match into an ashtray and unrolled a map on his desk and leaned to study it, undisturbed. There was a shade of pink colour along the right side of his lower face, as though from a blow.

CHAPTER EIGHT

EUCHRED AGAIN

MacDonald, first man to appear on the job each morning, was also the last man to depart in the evening. Usually, he sat the last fifteen minutes on the porch outside the office recapitulating the day's accomplishments. Sometimes with a tepid tin of beer from a small, private closet in his office, and maybe with his pipe going as well, for although MacDonald was not a heavy smoker by any means, he enjoyed tobacco under some conditions, and when he was alone after the work-day had ended, the pipe was a pleasant companion, like the beer.

But this particular evening he had neither the smoke nor the beer. In fact, he didn't even need that moment to himself, because while the telephone had rung as often as ever, he had been shielded from its annoyance. Now, he was finished for the day, and the last hour he hadn't been interrupted at all, so instead of waiting for his private moment alone, he'd already had it.

He had not seen Patricia Tolman again that day, after the interlude of the culvert—which had arrived hours before quitting time, had been checked for proper size, found suitable, and dumped. When the annoyed straw-boss who had wanted it, saw the pile on his way out of the development at quitting time, he turned and threw a casual salute at MacDonald.

Finally, there was the matter of getting Patricia Tolman back to the lodge. His real quandary was not her transportation—there were half a dozen car-owning roughnecks outside finding a dozen excuses for delaying their departure for the day, which none had ever done before, obviously eager to help. His real quandary was how to handle her now that her grandfather was ill.

It was hardly gallant to kick her off the job under those circumstances. And yet, if he didn't explain why he just might tolerate her for a few more days, it would undoubtedly appear to her as though he had decided she was valuable after all. And of course she wasn't. Anyone could take those damned telephone calls. Even that college kid he'd been using around the office, could have done as well with the culvert pipe.

And where, incidentally, *was* that college

boy?

MacDonald strode out on to the front gallery and watched the workmen stream past, some dirtier than others, all grinning slyly as they saw him up there. When the surveying crew appeared he called to the bushy-haired, youngest member, and beckoned. When the collegian stopped in front of the verandah, MacDonald said, 'I thought you'd be working in the office today.'

The young man's eyes widened. 'Two of us in there?'

'What do you mean?'

'The new secretary—Miss Tolman—and me, both? There isn't that much work, Mister MacDonald. And the survey crew is short-handed.'

Mac's temple began to throb. He gave himself time for the anger to pass by bending to knock dottle from the pipe against the heel of his boot. Then he said, 'Look, let *me* decide whether there's not enough work or not, will you?'

'Yes sir. Well, do you want me in the office tomorrow?'

Mac peered into his pipe. 'No,' he growled. 'Stay with the survey crew.' He didn't look up until the collegian was happily hastening back to the car he'd ride down to the village in. It didn't help any either, when MacDonald saw the other young men in that car listening intently to what the collegian was telling them.

Finally, even the hopefuls who expected Patricia to appear, in need of a ride down, had to give up and also depart, and when the dust had settled behind the last car MacDonald sighed and turned—and found himself facing her in the office doorway.

'I'll be leaving now, Mister MacDonald, if there's nothing else . . .'

He turned, scanned the empty yard where only his own car sat in the early, forest twilight, turned back and said, 'Where did you park? Where is your car?'

'I don't have one up here. I didn't bring it.'

'And how will you get down to the village?'

'Walk. It's only about two miles.'

Mac looked as though he would groan—or curse. He did neither, actually. He might have except that she told him she'd put four messages on his desk; they were from people who wanted him to call them back about matters that seemed to require his special, personal attention. Then she stepped through the doorway and eased past him down the broad, low steps.

'Wait a minute,' he exclaimed. 'You'll ride back with me.'

'Mister MacDonald, I enjoy walking. Particularly up here where the air is so fragrant.' She was looking up at him, as unsmiling as she'd been all day long.

He frowned. 'You can't just go walking around this time of day. Maybe you're in the

70

woods, but it's still not a smart thing to do. And by the time you got down there it'd be dark.'

He turned, locked the outer office door, remembered how she'd got in that morning and after balancing the thought briefly of hiking round back to also lock that door, he decided it wasn't worth it. She'd be back in the morning as sure as the sun would rise, and it did not appear beyond her to fling a rock through a window to get in if he locked her out, and anyway . . . oh the hell with it!

As he turned back and saw her still watching him, he motioned towards his dusty car. She shook her head. 'No thanks. I'd rather walk.'

He interpreted that as he was sure she had meant it. 'Look, I'm *asking* you to ride back with me. Is that better?'

'It's worse. You're being so fatherly it's disgusting.'

He stepped off the last step. 'If you're going to hang around, someone'll have to be fatherly, you know.'

'No, I don't know. And now that it's quitting time and you're just another man, not the boss, I'll tell you something else. You're not the fatherly type.'

'I'm damned near that much older than you are,' he retorted.

'In a pig's eye you are,' she flared out at him. 'You're thirty or thirty-one. I'm almost twenty-three. How many seven- or eight-year-old fathers have you known?' She turned towards the dusty roadway.

He said, 'Wait,' but she kept on walking and did not even look back. He swore under his breath, went over to his car, jammed it into gear and started after her. When he drew alongside he said, 'I've never seen any seven-year old fathers. Now let *me* ask *you* a question: How many hungry bears have *you* seen?'

She hesitated, but only briefly, and started walking straight on again. 'I don't frighten that easily, Mister MacDonald. Bears don't come round where people are.'

He groaned aloud. 'What do you think is the reason they keep their garbage bins down in the village chained to the buildings then? Bears come down every blasted night, and they are no more afraid of people than lap-dogs. But they aren't above knocking you around a bit if they're hungry and cross, and you happen to be between them and where they want to get. Now get into this car.'

She stopped and turned. 'You're trying to scare me.'

'Miss Tolman . . . If I gave you my solemn oath . . . Look; just ride back with me this one time. And tonight go ask around the lodge about the local bears. If I'm lying you'll never have to ride with me again. I promise that. Now get in here.'

She got in. As he eased the car ahead she

looked ruefully at the heavy layer of dust on her shoes and ankles. Summertime in the mountains, enjoyable though it might be, also meant dust and dirt, and constant bathing.

She sat well away from him as she said, 'Incidentally, I know what made you change your mind this afternoon.'

'I didn't change it. If you mean about having you around, I haven't changed it, and I'm not likely to change it.' He looked over at her suddenly. 'What do you mean, you know why?'

'I telephoned home this afternoon to have some clothes and things sent up. I was told about grandfather's heart attack.'

'Oh. Well . . .'

'Mister MacDonald, didn't you see through that? He knew today would be the critical period in our relationship. You would hit the ceiling. I'd want to come home. Both of us would telephone him and raise the roof. So, naturally, he couldn't be reached, and probably the best way to accomplish that was to be too ill.'

Mac drove for a half mile without speaking or taking his eyes off the road. His temple throbbed gently. When they topped out over a north-south ridge that intersected the east-west roadway, he disengaged gears, slowed to a halt with the panoramic view heat-hazed and breathtaking on ahead, and said, 'Do you know what I wish?'

'I'll guess. That my grandfather was fifty

years younger so you could punch him in the nose.'

'No. I wish I'd never even heard the Tolman name.'

She looked at the hands in her lap and softly said, 'Mister MacDonald, don't you suppose that all through my grandfather's life people have got just this angry at him? So—he anticipates everything they will do because he's been through it over and over.'

'It's a wonder someone hasn't throttled him.'

'That's not the way.'

'What is? Quit?'

'Of course not. That's childish. Like a pouting little kid.' She lifted her blue eyes and smiled at him. 'Will you let me help you?'

They sat gazing at one another a long moment before he jerked the car into gear and rolled forward again. 'No! I don't trust you one damned bit more than I trust that grandfather of yours!'

She lapsed back into solemn silence. When he halted in the space reserved for his car, out beside the lodge, she alighted. 'Well, I should thank you for the ride, but it'd be hypocrisy on my part. Anyway, it's been an interesting day.'

He sat in the car watching her walk away. She had a supple, rather athletic stride, and he *did* like short, curly hair.

He let her get out of sight before leaving the car and heading for his own quarters on the

74

second floor. Under a stinging shower-head he thought about what she'd said. No question about it, if anyone knew that antiquated old devil well enough to get the best of him, it would be her.

He turned red all over again, thinking how he'd been duped. The damned old monster had even fooled a medical doctor, his own son, his daughter-in-law, and even the blasted servants.

If that should have made MacDonald feel a little better, being only one of many people who had been duped, it did not do so. As he was getting dressed in fresh suntans for dinner downstairs, he thought only of how he, *himself*, had been euchred—again.

'Quit,' he told himself. 'The hell with what that rich girl with reddish hair and the long legs thinks!' He was still muttering when he went out into the long hallway, bound for the downstairs dining-room, and was intercepted by the scowling straw-boss of the early morning. Now, the man, also freshly scrubbed and shiny, beamed.

'Mac, you sure got results on the damned culvert. I was beginning to think that gal had you off schedule. Like maybe you was slipping a little, after bein' so efficient up to now.'

MacDonald turned on the man with a fierce oath.

'That damned girl and her diabolical old grandfather are the bane of my life. I wish to hell you had her in your damned road-building crew!'

MacDonald flung forward and went stamping along towards the stair-well, while behind him stood a perfectly paralysed straw-boss whose eyebrows had climbed so high they were nearly lost in his hairline.

Behind him a dozen or so doors, a calm, quiet voice said, 'I'll apologise for him. He's a very unpleasant man, and if that isn't bad enough, he just doesn't know when someone is trying to help him. The big lout!'

The straw-boss, caught in a verbal barrage of cross-fire, said, 'Yes ma'm, whatever you say,' and ducked off down that same stair-well. 'Brother! Wait until the lads hear about *this*, over at the beer-hall tonight!'

CHAPTER NINE

MORE VISITORS

The following afternoon Patricia's father and mother arrived, bringing the clothing and other personal effects she'd telephoned about. It was the first time her mother had seen the development, and only the second time for her father.

MacDonald was in a meeting with his straw-bosses and came out only long enough to welcome them both, ask Patricia to show them around, and put a Land-Rover at their disposal if they cared to drive back through the forest where the final roads were being built, the final division of acreage into sites, was under way.

As soon as MacDonald had returned to his meeting Elyse looked worriedly at her daughter. 'Isn't he rather rough and crude, dear? I mean—he's so brusque, so large and domineering.'

'Mother, that's what it takes to do this job. Actually he's very efficient and knowledgeable.'

Her father, standing by a window, turned slowly. 'And honest, Patricia? It seems to me there is an awful lot of pipe and equipment up here. Have you studied the depreciation schedules yet to determine how much is lost?'

Patrica did not answer her father's question, but she showed a little hostility. 'Two-thirds of the project is completed. If there'd been anything unusual going on, believe me, by now Grandfather would have known about it. By the way, how is Grandfather?'

'He's resting better today,' intoned her father, turning back to gaze out of the window again. 'It was a mild seizure. But of course, in a man his age . . . By the way, Patricia, we brought your things. They're out in the car. Why didn't you bring them along when you came up here to work, and was there some

77

specific reason why you preferred not telling your mother and me this was your intention?'

She had to force a smile because her mother was looking at her. 'Well . . . it was a kind of spur-of-the-moment thing, Dad.'

Elyse smiled pithily. 'Are you sure, sweetheart, that Grandfather Tolman didn't get you up here, then talk you into staying? That would be so very much like him, you know.'

Her father turned. 'Elyse!'

To keep this from blowing up into something, Patricia headed for the door with a cheery little gesture for her parents to follow along. Neither of them were dressed for Land-Roving and Patricia had never before driven one of the bronco-like vehicles, but with her parents tucked safely in the back seat and a filtered, fragrant afternoon of sunlight driving up ahead, she fought her way through the gears and drove them over roads that were graded, bevelled for drainage, gravelled, and dusty.

The development was less than a square mile, and if that did not in some respects seem like very much land, when one inspected it from all the little roadways leading to individual areas, in and out among giant pines over culverted creeks that showed the shadowy dark flash of trout, taking over an hour to do all this, it seemed in fact to be a quite extensive development.

By the time Patricia returned to the office with her parents, the conference inside had broken up and MacDonald was talking on a telephone in a loud and bruising tone of voice. Patricia, leading her parents inside, winked as though MacDonald's rudeness were amusing. Neither of her parents winked back.

She got them both a chilled coke and said as soon as they'd got the dust from their throats, she'd see them down to the lodge. Only when they mentioned remaining overnight before starting back, was she dubious.

MacDonald came forth into the front room and asked how the development looked. Patricia's mother answered with a little vague smile, that it seemed to be very impressive. Her father was a bit more candid. 'How much longer before the work is finished, Mister MacDonald, and the selling begins?'

'A month,' said Mac. 'Barring delays. If everything goes as it's been doing lately, we might even be able to shave a few days—maybe even a full week—off that schedule.' MacDonald threw himself into a nearby chair, looked from Patricia to her parents, and offered a little wry smile. 'I've already begun calling for completion billings from the companies we won't be patronizing any longer. It's the preliminary phase of closing out this end of it. Of course as soon as the crews move out, the sales staff will move into this office.' He studied Patricia's father. 'That's your answer. How sales go isn't my cup of tea, Mister Tolman.' He straightened in the chair, looking from Elyse to her husband, and when neither of them spoke, he shot up to his feet. 'I've got to go over to the lakeside area. Miss Tolman, why don't you take your parents down to the village.'

Pat nodded. 'They plan to stay overnight, then drive back in the morning, Mister MacDonald.'

He looked thoughtfully at her. 'I see. You've explained about accommodation?'

'No sir. We hadn't got around to that.'

He continued to gaze at Patricia. She thought she saw the irritation in his stare she'd come to know quite well by now. She also thought she knew the reason for it. 'I'd have telephoned around if I'd known they were coming in so late today.'

He nodded, ironically, she was sure. 'Well, go on down with them and see what you can dig up.' MacDonald smiled at the older people. 'Good luck. I'll probably see you again, but if I don't, I'm glad you came up and had a look around. You might, if you would, tell Mister Tolman Senior I'd like very much to drop down and have a conference with him—when he's up to it, of course.'

Patricia's parents rose looking slightly the worse for wear after the Land-Rover ride, particularly her mother who was fragile at best. Her father, shaking MacDonald's hand, said, 'I have no idea when my father will be on his feet again. Heart trouble at his age in life is very serious.'

'Yes,' murmured MacDonald. 'People in their eighties have to be extremely careful.'

Davey Tolman coloured a little and looked very pained, but he only nodded at MacDonald, then ushered his wife and daughter out on to the verandah and down towards his cream-coloured Cadillac. At the last minute Patricia made an excuse to rush back inside. She'd forgot her handbag. That was only part of it. She got the handbag, then she went to the open doorway of MacDonald's office, watched him light his pipe, then said, 'Aren't you terribly clever today. That was an unnecessary barb—about Grandfather Tolman being in his eighties. Why be mean to my father? He's never done anything to you.'

Through smoke MacDonald said, 'He's a Tolman, isn't he?'

Patricia clenched her fists, made an inarticulate sound in her throat, whirled and ran from the office. As soon as she was gone MacDonald reached for the telephone and dialled Crestline Lodge. As soon as the manager came on MacDonald said, 'Frank, Miss Tolman's parents are up. They expect to spend the night before heading back to the city. They'll have to have accommodation.'

The answer came back in tones of genuine anguish. 'For God's sake, Mac, why do you do these things to me? I don't even have a broom-closet available.'

'One double-bed for one night, Frank.'

'It might as well be the Presidential suite for a year. Mac, I swear to you, there isn't an unoccupied bed in the whole blasted lodge. I've been referring tourists to the motor inns for the past two weeks. I've even been sending them on down to Bakersfield.'

'You dug up accommodation for their daughter. How about putting a bed in her sitting-room, just for tonight?'

'Mac, I don't have the bed. I don't even have a sleeping-bag on the premises. Look, you know damned well after all the business you've brought me, if I could do it for anyone, I'd do it for you. But I give you my word—'

'I've got the solution, Frank. Go up to my rooms, take my shaving stuff out, have clean sheets put on the bed, and when they get down there, turn the rooms over to them—without mentioning me at all. Okay?'

'Where will you sleep?'

'Here, in the office on the job, I guess. There's a bedroll up here, and for one night it shouldn't be too bad. I'll be down for supper though, and to get my shaving stuff.'

Frank was agreeable, in a worried, harassed way. When MacDonald rang off he laughed. Frank was one of those people who developed ulcers by thirty, grey hair by forty, and dropped dead at fifty. Life, in MacDonald's view, was a serious business, but not that serious, and even he, in one of his most exasperated moments on the job, let off steam in anger, then rationalized his way out of difficulties.

As for sleeping in the office, he'd slept in lots of worse places in his lifetime. He went to search for that sleeping-bag someone had stored in a closet—he did not even remember who put it there—and when it was located he dragged it forth, kicked the dust from it and carried it into his private office where there was a couch. This idea did not pan out; both the sleeping-bag and MacDonald were too long for the couch. He dumped it on the floor and forgot it when the telephone rang.

The call was from Los Angeles. Some associate of Tolman Junior's was trying to reach him, and had been referred to the Crestline development office by the servants at the Brentwood estate. MacDonald told the man to try Crestline Lodge, and rang off.

Five minutes later his road-foreman came stamping in, wet, disgusted and muddy. In pushing a grade below road level to make a bed for sub-surface chat, then rock, and finally blacktop surfacing, his crew had opened up a seam of creek water. Mac told the foreman to have culvert trucked to the site. He then used the inter-job transceiver to reach his heavy-equipment boss, and ordered a D-8 'dozer back to clear a trench for the culvert, lower the pipe into place, and cover it, diverting the

83

water beneath the roadway.

It was one of the details his life was made up of. Nothing very frustrating, providing he had everything on hand that would be needed. And he had it, even the culvert-pipe, although he did not dwell on how that happened to be. Finally, because part of his job had to do with cajoling diplomacy, he raided his secret cache of two beers, gave one to the disgusted foreman, had one himself, and sat for a few minutes with the foreman, making small-talk, until the beer had done what talking by itself never actually did: Got the road-foreman back into a reasonably pleasant frame of mind before he went hiking out to drive back to his job.

The balance of this day MacDonald had to answer the blasted telephone no less than eleven times, and eight of those times the callers were either eager-beaver estate agents wanting to know when, and if, they could start hauling up prospective site-purchasers, or else they were honey-toned salesmen peddling, at enormous savings of course, everything from ready-mix cement or pipe, to bunting and printed flags to be set up along the roadway leading to the development.

MacDonald, after one day, the previous one, of having all these people filtered through Patricia's hands and kept out of his schedule, admitted privately that there was an advantage to having someone with tact and a quick wit, in the office. That college boy he'd tried using had simply answered those calls, then put them all on MacDonald's line, which was no better than not answering the calls at all.

The day closed, eventually, with nothing unusual or particularly disastrous—including the exposed vein of creek water—occurring, and when the crews knocked off at quitting time, MacDonald went forth to listen to the usual comments, suggestions, and gripes, then, when everyone was gone, he retreated to his cache, got another can of beer, and went forth as he'd formerly done, to sit in forest-stillness on the verandah, and have the pleasant moment to himself.

He was mellow before half the beer was downed. He even smiled ruefully as he considered Old Man Tolman's fake heart attack. The smile became slightly strained as he also reflected upon giving up his rooms for the night. If there were two things he looked forward to at the close of each working day, they were his shower and his rest.

Finally, with an appetite sharpened by the beer, MacDonald rose to rid himself of the empty beer can, and to afterwards stroll out to his car for the drive down to Crestline Village for dinner. He would probably meet the Tolmans down there again, and if he didn't exactly look forward to that, at least it did not enter his mind to ask them to take their confounded daughter back with them.

CHAPTER TEN

A SUDDEN STORM

He met them again. At least he met Tolman
Junior, who was brooding in the cool bar—
called the 'Redwood Room' although no
redwood trees grew within seven hundred
miles of Crestline Village—when MacDonald
went there to buy a Scotch and soda. He
wouldn't have intruded on Tolman's privacy,
at the little table near a front window, even
then, if Tolman had not seen him and
beckoned him over, offering a chair.

Tolman's drink was a martini. Exactly
suitable to the Brentwood ethos, but out of
context in a room full of suntanned, noisy
loggers, heavy-equipment operators, and bull-
voiced foremen.

Tolman said, 'You know, after three drinks I
start feeling sorry for myself. This is my fourth
one.' He still forgot to smile, and his eyes were
dark with introspection. 'I envy those men of
yours over at the bar. As a young man I always
had some notion I'd be capable of building
roads and flattening forests.'

'Ever take a crack at it?' asked MacDonald,
sipping his drink and watching the older man's
shadowed face.

'No. And I didn't even turn out to be very

86

good at handling the financial and planning end either.'

'Maybe that's why?'

'What do you mean?'

'Well, a man pretty well knows what he ought to do with his life by the time he's twenty-five or thirty. If he does something else, he usually doesn't have his whole heart in it.'

Davey Tolman drained his glass, pushed it away and lit a cigarette. MacDonald watched all this with interest. He hadn't known the younger Tolman smoked, but then he did not know the younger Tolman very well in any case.

'Someday, Mister MacDonald,' growled the older man, 'I'm going to tackle something like this. On my own.'

'Like what, Mister Tolman?'

'Dammit, what are we talking about! The development. I'm going to find myself a piece of bare land and ramrod the whole damned thing myself. Well, maybe with one engineer, but otherwise do it all myself.'

MacDonald considered his half-empty glass. Tolman was beginning to sound like a man who'd had more than four martinis. As for the frustration—there was no way under the sun, providing a man lived long enough and worked hard enough, not to experience *that*.

MacDonald said. 'There's an old saying I used to hear when I was a kid, Mister Tolman: Blacksmith stick to your anvil.'

The older man looked up. 'Finance isn't my anvil, MacDonald.' He leaned on the table. 'I'm past forty. Drinking martinis is fine for relaxation, but it gets awfully tiresome as a profession. Did you know that?'

'Sure,' replied MacDonald, and finished his Scotch-and soda. 'Any kind of inactivity gets damned tiresome.' He stood up and smiled at Tolman. 'If I can help you get started on that development project, I'll be glad to do it. Now I've got a good appetite. See you later. By the way, how is your accommodation?'

'Fine. It's someone's room who won't be in tonight.'

MacDonald nodded and strode out of the Redwood Room.

Patricia and her mother had a table in the dining-room somewhat apart from the other diners, which wasn't such a bad idea since construction workers, even when on their best behaviour, could be shockingly frank and colourful.

MacDonald got his usual table, a single because he chose to eat alone, and his usual meal; whatever happened to be the speciality of the kitchen each day. He was a very easy man to feed. He had no definite dislikes, only a few preferences.

He glanced over where the women were eating, only once or twice. The last time was when Tolman Junior came to join his women with the stride of a captain walking the high bridge in a moderately rough sea. He smiled to himself and finished his dinner, then went in search of the manager to get his shaving things, and anything else the manager had managed to salvage from MacDonald's rooms before the Tolmans had arrived.

The manager was gone for the evening, but an assistant took MacDonald to the lodge's office and got the battered old valise the manager had stowed MacDonald's effects in.

After he'd taken this out and flung it into his car, MacDonald returned to the verandah, nearly empty at this time of day while everyone was either at dinner or across the road at the tavern, and stoked up his pipe. It was always pleasant on the verandah in the early twilight. For that matter, it was usually pleasant anywhere a man found himself to be after dinner, after the day's work, this time of day.

He detected movement, eventually, and turned slightly to see who was approaching. It was Patricia and he sighed, lowered his pipe and nodded as she stepped around in front and perched upon the log railing in front of him, but slightly to his right. She gazed at him as though something troubled her. He was sure something did; he'd yet to be around her when something wasn't bothering her.

'Good dinner?' he asked, with false cheerfulness.

'Excellent. But then it usually is, isn't it? Why didn't you tell me you were going to give up your room tonight?'

He puffed a moment, then said, 'Recite me the law that says I have to tell you anything, Miss Tolman.'

She flushed. 'It wasn't necessary. Unless of course you wished to appear chivalrous to the Tolman heirs, Mister MacDonald.'

His neck began to redden. 'Do you know what the Tolman heirs can do, as far as I'm concerned, Miss Tolman?'

She kept looking at him, but when next she spoke she'd backed off a little. 'Is it essential to fight every time we meet, Mister MacDonald?'

'*I* don't start it. As for the room—they had to bed down somewhere, didn't they? The lodge was full.'

'The manager could have put a bed in my quarters.'

'He didn't have a bed to put in there! I asked him to do that. Or he thought of it and couldn't. I don't remember which. At any rate, why make such a federal case out of it? They needed a bed—they got one. I've got a sleeping-bag up at the office and there's running water, a heating element—and privacy.'

'Well, I came out to thank you.'

'You are very welcome!'

'I wish it wasn't against the law to cut your throat, Mister MacDonald,' said Patricia, jumping down from the railing. 'I also hope it rains tonight and washes out the roads up

90

there. Goodnight!'

He clamped the pipe between strong teeth and watched her march back towards the front door of the lodge. Then he discovered that the confounded pipe had lost its fire and banged it with unnecessary roughness upon the railing to empty it, and got to his feet. It wasn't even possible to relax on the blasted verandah of the lodge any more!

That road-foreman he'd given the beer to earlier came sauntering around the side of the building sucking loudly upon a toothpick, which he spat out when he saw MacDonald, and smiled.

'Mac; have you seen the barometer?' he asked.

MacDonald shook his head. He hadn't looked at the barometer in weeks.

'Rain,' said the foreman, and Mac looked slowly around towards the doorway through which Patricia had vanished. 'Rain sure as hell, Mac. Barometer's dropping and look at that sky. 'Course, if a good wind'd come up it might blow the clouds away, but I'm not betting on that either, even though it never rains in Southern California in midsummer—except high in the mountains like around here.'

MacDonald leaned out over the porch railing and scanned what could be seen of the sky. There were big, dirty old billowing clouds up there, moving inexorably in from the northwest, where most summer rains came

91

from, if they came at all.

The foreman leaned upon the nearest log—upright. He didn't seem over anxious, but then, being paid on an hourly scale and with no personal involvement in the development, there was no real reason for him to worry. 'We got that seam covered,' he exclaimed, 'so that's not likely to wash out. But up in the lakeside tract we got about a mile and a half of fresh-laid dirt that isn't compacted yet, and if it rains very hard you can bet your sweet bippy that's going to wash out.'

MacDonald said, 'What else?' in a tart tone of voice.

'Nothing much,' opined the foreman, fishing in a shirt-pocket for another toothpick. 'Anyway, we can't help any of it, can we?'

The foreman strolled away to join several men leaving the lodge grounds and heading across the road towards the tavern. MacDonald watched them for a moment, with some vague urge to join them and maybe take on a load, but he didn't. He wasn't really a very successful drinker even when he wasn't worried, but like now, raising his eyes to study the gathering black clouds again, he forgot about the urge and began going over in his mind's eye, all the areas up at the development that could be injured by a heavy rainstorm.

Finally, no longer in the mood for watching people and listening to them, he went out to the car, climbed in and drove off heading up the road for the development office.

He wasn't paying any attention to the car so when it made a more than customary shudder after striking one of the roadway ruts, he simply corrected the steering and drove into the next rut. That time, the wheel came off. He saw it in the glare of headlamps going its independent way on a wobbly course out across the pavement, down over a low bank, and past several trees until it struck one, bounded back, and toppled over.

He got out and bent to examine the front-end, now resting at a crippled angle on the axle. That was when the first fat raindrop struck his shirt. Evidently the wheel had been loose a long while, because by using a match and running fingertips over the lug-bolts, he could easily discern the stripped-down smoothness where each lug should have been threaded.

It was not an unheard-of accident although it was the first time anything like this had ever happened to MacDonald, and while he could squat there on the deserted road for as long as he wished, nothing short of a tow-car and a complete new set of threaded lug-bolts could put the car back on all four wheels again.

Another fat raindrop struck him. This time on the back of the neck, and it was both large and cold, which brought his attention back to the dark environment.

He was not actually more than three-quarters of a mile from the lodge, so when he rose, exasperated to the point of selective and sizzling profanity over such a stupid event, he simply turned back down the slight incline and walked off, leaving the crippled car where it sat. It was off to the side of the road so it would not impede morning traffic, but even if it had been in the middle of the road he couldn't have done anything about it. Threewheeled cars were about as functional as three-legged horses.

Three more big fat raindrops struck MacDonald, simultaneously this time, so he stopped to look upwards. Those great black clouds had finally, in the leisurely but immutable manner of thunderheads, come all together. Now, with the overhead heavens full of them, and with no place for them to move to, they began pushing up against one another, squeezing water out a little at a time.

MacDonald resumed his hike, but now he became more brisk about it, because the rain was finally beginning to come steadily. Not very heavily, at first, even though the size of the droplets was large, but with a consistency that indicated, by the time he could reach the lodge, the world would be under heavy attack.

He could see the lights down at Crestline but as he hastened along they became increasingly blurred. Also, he became increasingly drenched. And that water was as cold as ice. Elsewhere, at much lower elevations, these summer showers were delightful and welcome, and warm. But not above three thousand feet. MacDonald was shivering before he slogged the last three hundred yards down to the lodge. Shivering and as wet as he'd ever been. The village, lit though it was at this relatively early hour, was empty of the usual strollers. Even the verandah of the lodge was deserted.

A glistening, great bus stood before the lodge. Evidently there were icing conditions on the far slope of the Grapevine, and the driver had taken refuge, with his passengers, inside the lodge. If this were so, then even that broom-closet the manager had mentioned earlier would have sleeping people crammed into it like sardines.

MacDonald didn't even bother going the extra few hundred feet around front. He headed for the nearest overhanging rooftop, which happened to be the one projecting out over the service-porch and the huge kitchen. But even after he was in that blessed shelter, water still ran inside his shirt from his rain-matted hair.

CHAPTER ELEVEN

UNEXPECTED TOGETHERNESS

MacDonald's guess about the bus-passengers had been correct. Not only had the lodge been full to capacity prior to the sudden storm, but after the arrival of those bewildered and hapless travellers, sixty in number, there were cots and blankets, and even old rugs brought forth from storage, put everywhere it was possible to find the room for people to lie down.

MacDonald's wet and shivering appearance in the kitchen only inspired one of the serving staff who knew who he was, to bring him a mug of hot coffee and ask if his car had broken down, which seemed rather obvious since he was back again after driving off, and had obviously hoofed it back as well.

He'd left the valise in the car otherwise his belongings were upstairs in his room, where the Tolmans were probably blissfully sleeping to the pleasant sound of rain on the roof. He asked about dry clothing and was told that as far as anyone knew every usable stitch had already been commandeered by others who had also got wet.

Feeling better with hot coffee under his belt, he considered what had to be done.

Obviously, to preclude the likelihood of influenza or at the very least a case of sniffles, he had to get into dry clothing, and just as obviously he could hardly march upstairs and barge into his room to get those dry clothes after having been so cavalier about giving up his room.

But there was someone who could barge in, up there.

He climbed the back stairs to the second floor and when he'd located Patricia's room did not hesitate to bang on the door. When that brought no immediate results he banged again. It was the third time that there was a response. A voice sounding surprisingly unsleepy asked who it was and what they wanted.

He answered in a growl. 'You could open the door and find out, unless you think it's Black Bart.'

She opened the door and looked at him. She didn't look as though she'd even been to bed although she obviously had because of the bed gown and robe. Her eyes went down him, then up. 'What in the world happened to you, Mister MacDonald?'

'What does it look like? I got rained on.'

'But you were supposed to be up at the office.'

'I know where I was supposed to be! The car lost a wheel about a mile up the road. I walked back. Now if that is satisfactory, I wonder if you would go down to my room, go

97

into the front closet, locate some fresh suntans and bring them down here to me.'

Patricia opened the door wider. 'Certainly. I'm sorry I kept you standing like this. Look, there's an electric heater in the bathroom, why don't you go and stand by it while I'm gone?'

As she moved past he held out a hand. 'You can't just walk through the door, you know. Take the key.'

When she had gone he cocked his head at the sound of rain on the roof. It did not seem to be as strong as before, or perhaps it was muted by some kind of dead-air space between the roof and the ceiling above his head.

He entered her rooms, passed through the dim light to the small, tiled bathroom, and found the electric heater. She evidently was one of those people who slept with windows open because as he passed through the darkened bedroom he saw the curtains dancing over near the balcony, and the room was chilly.

The heat felt good and its red glow was cheerful. He placed his back to it and felt round for his pipe. It was there in his pocket and so was his pouch, but the tobacco was hopelessly damp and his matches had soggily disintegrated.

It didn't matter. He probably should not smoke in Patricia Tolman's rooms anyway. He turned to look out of a small nearby window, but all that was visible of the night was probably the same view a fish had from inside a dirty fishbowl. There was no wind, or if there was he could not hear it and he would have felt better if there had been, at least it might have broken up the steadily hammering downpour.

He thought of the development, and gave his head a slight shake.

But to be fair, he had been terribly lucky up until now, and had actually gained a little on the completion date. So perhaps it was about time for a rainstorm, or some other natural disaster, to come along.

At the worst he would have to go back and re-work perhaps a couple of miles of road-bed surface. Otherwise, there wouldn't be too much damage. And in another way it was a good thing that the storm had come when it did. This way, with a tremendous amount of water suddenly dumped over everything, he and his straw-bosses would know whether all their calculations were on the safe side. For example, they had sunk an awful lot of culvert to carry off surplus rain— and snow-water. By tomorrow, providing the storm ended soon, they would know if the drainage system was adequate.

'Mister MacDonald . . . ?'

He roused himself, turned and peeked out of the bathroom door. Patricia was out there in the gloom of her airy bedroom holding something forward. He reached.

'Don't you even know where you keep your own clothing?' she said, handing everything to him. 'You said the front closet. These things were in the dresser in the bedroom. There was nothing in the front closet but a bunch of books, and some other junk.'

'Okay,' he said. 'I'm sorry. I wasn't too clear, was I?'

He closed the door on her and began shedding his soggy things. The bathroom was a bit too warm now, with no ventilation and that cheery-glowing heater still working at maximum capacity. He turned it off, then had to switch on the overhead light to dispel the darkness.

Getting dressed did not take long. It required more time to sort things from one set of pockets to the other set. Then he opened the door, flicked off the light and said, 'Miss Tolman . . . ?'

She did not answer. Obviously, since the bed was turned back, she was not there. He walked forth and called a little louder. This time he got an answer from the outer room. 'Coffee, Mister MacDonald?' She was dressed, after a fashion, in a loose sweater and tan slacks, but she still wore bedroom slippers.

She smiled as he came out of the bedroom looking crisp and fresh, his soggy clothing in one hand. He said, 'Coffee?'

Her smile was beguiling. 'While you were getting dressed I trotted downstairs and raided the kitchen. It ought to take the last chill out of you.'

'That was very thoughtful of you, Miss Tolman.' He might have mentioned already being awash with coffee that he'd got only a short while earlier, but he didn't. When she held out the cup, he returned her smile.

'You ought to smile more often, Mister MacDonald. It makes you very handsome.'

He tasted the coffee and found that it had been smoothed out with a few drops of cream. 'I'll try to remember,' he told her, 'because I've always wanted to be very handsome.'

Her smile winked out. 'Do you simply *have* to be so sarcastic? I was only trying to be pleasant.'

'I wasn't being sarcastic, Miss Tolman. It was a joke.'

'A joke?' She stared at him. 'I've heard the Scots had a lousy sense of humour, Mister MacDonald. Now I believe it! Some joke!'

He went to a window near the front balcony and peered upwards at the dripping sky as he said, in an indifferent tone, 'Young lady, don't judge Scots by me. My mother was English, my grandmother was Irish, and I had a great-grandmother who was German.' He turned back, grinning. 'Only the name is still Scottish. Okay, it was a poor joke. I apologise.' He kept gazing at her. 'You don't even have to smile to be handsome.' He seemed slightly startled at himself. 'But of course you already know that,

I'm sure.' He walked forward with the half empty cup in his hand. 'The rain is easing up.'

'Will there be a lot of damage at the development?'

'Probably.' He finished the coffee, leaned to put the cup aside, and shot her a rueful look. 'No one has good luck all the time. Anyway, we're still two-thirds of the way along, so some delay won't kill us. Uh—Miss Tolman, I appreciate you getting the clothes for me. And the coffee. And the use of the bathroom to change in.' He paused, concentrating. 'Oh yes—and for being kind enough to get out of bed to help a damp wayfarer in the night.'

She almost smiled at him, not quite but almost. He was clearly trying to be pleasant and courteous now; to smooth over his bad image with her. 'What about the car?' she asked. 'Is it wrecked?'

'No. I'll send someone back to fix it tomorrow. Now I'd better go and bed down.'

'Where, Mister MacDonald?'

He considered that. 'A good question, Miss Tolman. I'll find a place.'

She pointed towards a large sofa over near the balcony windows. 'I'll get you a blanket.' She was already moving briskly towards her own room when he stopped her. 'No thanks. Look, I appreciate it very much. You've been wonderful. But this just isn't right, you see, and anyway I can find—'

'I'll get you a blanket, Mister MacDonald,'

she interrupted to say, rather flatly and annoyedly. 'And if you have a dirty mind it's not my fault.'

'A dirty mind! Why damn it all, Miss Tolman...'

She had passed from his sight into her bedroom. Moments later she returned with a wadded-up woollen blanket which she tossed over to him.

'Mister MacDonald, please don't snore,' she said, and stood in her bedroom doorway gazing out at him as though it were the most natural thing in the world for him to sleep on her sofa, which as a matter of fact it was this particular night because there was no other suitable place in the entire lodge.

'Goodnight,' she said, closing her door half way. 'You really astonish me, Mister MacDonald, I'd have thought you were a— well—a bold, brassy man. One of those swashbuckling Errol Flynn types.' She closed the door.

He repeated that name. 'Errol Flynn?' Joseph MacDonald was not a movie fan. He turned and looked over at the large, inviting sofa. He was tired; that heat on his back had loosened nerves and muscles. It was very late now, past midnight, and the alternative to the sofa and blanket was a pallet on the kitchen floor, probably, sleeping cheek-by-jowl to some total stranger.

He went to the sofa, kicked off his boots,

tested the sofa's cushions and measured its length, found both satisfactory, and lay back with the blanket over him. Even his own bed didn't feel this good. At least he didn't recall it feeling so soft and warm, but then he seldom heeded beds, he slept in them, used them and ignored them.

Tired as he was, sleep would not come right away. Ghostly in the watery gloom of the sitting-room was the mound of his mud-splattered, soggy clothing over by the front door. Nearer were their two coffee cups, side by side on a little end-table.

He glanced at her closed bedroom door. She was really sweet. Pretty as a picture and sweet. He turned up on his side, grunted at himself, and closed his eyes.

Overhead, wind curved over the peaked rooftop and slid noisily down the long troughs above the caves. It carried sheets of fine raindrops in half a dozen different directions. Sounds of dripping water came from all sides, and although MacDonald did not notice, a vaporous pale light glowed now and then as tattered clouds parted to permit the moon to show through.

A fresh chill arrived and MacDonald dimly felt that, rolled the blanket tighter around himself and snuggled deeper into the yielding comfort of the sofa.

Stars came, eventually, as the scudding old clouds, flapping empty and racing southward ahead of the wind, broke away from the pine forest. On the highest peaks there was a light skiff of snow that would vanish as soon as morning sunlight arrived, but for the rest of that disorganized night whenever wind sped across those snowfields, then swooped over the village on its southward run, the cold increased a few degrees.

CHAPTER TWELVE

CONFRONTATION

MacDonald opened his eyes only when bright sunlight beat across his face. It took something like ten seconds for him to become oriented. The ceiling was unfamiliar, as was the sofa he was lying on, the room he was in, and finally, the quiet voice that said, 'The lion of Tolman acres returns to the living.'

He reared up, puckered his eyes and saw her standing over near the balcony windows looking amused. She was wearing a handsome thick sweater over a pale blouse, and a functional tweed skirt. It was summertime somewhere, but it didn't feel very much like it in her sitting-room at that moment, even though she had closed the windows and had switched on an electric wall-heater.

He sat up, ran both hands through his hair,

105

and felt embarrassed as he groped for his boots and tugged them on, then he stood up.

She pointed to her bedroom door. 'There is a fresh blade in the razor, Mister MacDonald, a fresh Turkish towel on the rack by the shower, and sorry as I am to have to offer it, a bar of scented soap.'

He looked over her shoulder where sunshine was making the soggy world outside glisten and sparkle. Anticipating his thoughts she reported that she had already been downstairs, and except for everything having run-off-water gurgling hither and yon, their world was as clean as though it had been scrubbed, and every speck of dust had been settled.

'By the time we've had breakfast it should be warm enough not to need a sweater. If you like I'll go down and order while you shower and shave. All right?'

He nodded. Her dazzling good looks and brisk efficiency had him slightly off-balance; he was not completely awake yet. She walked across to the door, turned and said, 'Good morning, Mister MacDonald.'

He understood. 'Sorry. It takes a bit of getting used to, Miss Tolman, being awakened by sunshine in a strange woman's room, and finding her all dazzling and witty before I've even washed my face.' He smiled back. 'Good morning to you, Miss Tolman.'

She departed and MacDonald shuffled off

to the bathroom to shower and shave, and gradually assume the appearance as well as the feel of a human being again.

He finished, ultimately, with a little smile. Whatever he had initially thought of Patricia Tolman—spoilt brat of a rich family with too much of everything, come to his job as a harbinger of trouble, dissention and unpleasantness—he had to admit now that she might still be some of those things, but she certainly wasn't unpleasant. Nor had she caused dissension, except between the two of them, and because MacDonald was a fair man, he admitted that this had been mostly his own fault.

He walked forth from the bathroom smelling a little more of violets—or was it roses?—than he'd have ordinarily smelled, and stepped out of her bedroom on his way out of the suite, and came face to face with Mister and Mrs. Davey Tolman, standing in their daughter's sitting-room with the hallway-door open at their backs. They had stopped in to invite her to have breakfast with them before they left for home.

No one moved for several moments. MacDonald's little kindly smile curdled under the astonished stares of the Tolmans, then Elyse Tolman, with a little, pitiful bleat, sank into a chair and her husband lost his colour.

MacDonald turned red, which annoyed him since he had actually done nothing, regardless of their thoughts, to blush about. He said, 'Your daughter is downstairs in the dining-room. I just used the shower. Got caught out last night with a disabled car and had to walk back in the storm. She—helped me.'

Elyse Tolman rolled her eyes to her husband. 'You see, Davey, I *did* see Patricia furtively going through that dresser last night. It wasn't a dream or my imagination. And I was right when I told you it was his room, too. It was no accident that his name was in that engineering book.'

David Tolman found his voice, eventually, and it matched the coldly hostile expression in his eyes. 'Mister MacDonald, it's offensive to Patricia's parents, finding you coming out of her bedroom.'

MacDonald's blush deepened. 'That insinuation is unwarranted, Mister Tolman. As you can see, your daughter isn't even here.'

'Look,' said Mrs. Tolman. 'Davey, look at the soiled clothing over by the door. He's wearing fresh things.' She rose and turned soulful eyes upon her husband. 'Take me out of here, David. Let's go home.'

Tolman kept studying MacDonald, white, and struggling with his control. 'You're fired,' he finally got out, his voice roughened by emotion. 'Pack up and get off the job, MacDonald!' He then led his wife out into the hallway and didn't even bother to close the door.

108

MacDonald saw the pile of damp clothing, realized how it had to look to Patricia's parents—and realized, too, how it had to look that she knew where to find his fresh suntans in the dresser, and said a coarse swear word out loud.

And now they would march downstairs and brace their daughter. Probably in front of whoever was in the dining-room. People as upset as the Tolmans were likely to make a terrible scene.

MacDonald left the room with a long stride, headed directly for the stairway and descended it two steps at a time. Several workmen, already on their way out, called a greeting or threw MacDonald a wave. He ignored everyone as he bore down upon the dining-room doorway. The workmen exchanged glances, then shrugged and kept on going.

Patricia was across the room at a table for two, but there was no sign of her parents. The dining-room manager came forward wearing his fixed smile. 'Miss Tolman has already ordered for you, Mister MacDonald and—'

'Where are her parents?' barked MacDonald, holding the man by the arm.

'Gone,' replied the surprised dining-room manager, as he worked his arm free. 'They checked out ten minutes ago. I guess they weren't hungry or they wanted to eat farther along.'

Mac relaxed slightly. 'Thanks,' he said, and

walked across to the table where Pat smiled upwards and pointed. A large platter of ham and eggs had just arrived at his place.

She said, pleased with herself, 'How's that for timing?'

He sat but did not even look downward. 'I was coming through the bedroom doorway on my way out—and your parents walked into the sitting-room.'

Patricia's expression gradually altered. At first, she looked a little baffled, then, as understanding came, she simply stared at him.

'I tried to explain that you weren't there, and that I'd got caught out in the storm last night.' He slumped in the chair still ignoring the platter in front of him. 'Your mother almost cried and your father fired me.'

'Fired you? You mean, fired you off the development job?'

'Yes.'

'Well, Mister MacDonald, didn't you explain?'

'Of course I explained,' he said loudly.

Her handsome brows dropped a notch and drew inward. 'I'm not hard of hearing. Keep your voice down unless you want to advertise this thing.'

'I was afraid they'd come in here and make some kind of scene with you.'

'My parents? Mister MacDonald, you don't know my mother and father.'

'Okay. I don't know your parents. But you'd

better come up with something, Miss Tolman. I can imagine how that had to look to them. Pretty awful. This whole blasted thing is going to drop on your shoulders.'

'*My* shoulders? Who was it who tried to help whom last night? And who was it who helped whom again this morning, even to scrounging a razor—*with* a new blade—and a fresh towel? What kind of a man *are* you, Mister MacDonald?'

'Now who's raising their voice,' he growled at her. 'All right. I'll do whatever I can. But you'll have to tell me, because I simply don't know how to make them believe nothing happened in that room last night.'

She was quiet for a moment, then pointed. 'Eat your breakfast before the eggs congeal and the ham gets cold. That's the first thing you have to do.'

'I'm not very hungry.'

'That doesn't matter, you will be before quitting time this evening.'

MacDonald started on his breakfast. She sat across from him gazing out of the window on her left. Not very far out there, near some blue-green young spruce trees, was where she'd slapped him. Eventually she said, 'Dad can't fire you. Only Grandfather can do that.'

He looked over. 'What's that got to do with it?'

'Enough,' she said, in a clipped tone of voice. 'When you've finished eating we'll drive

111

up to the job and get to work.'

'Aren't you going to try and get in touch with your folks?'

'How? They have no telephone in their car, and they'll be on the road most of the day. Anyway, Mister MacDonald, I'll need the time to figure out what I'll tell them.'

He blinked his surprise. 'The truth, of course.'

'Naturally the truth,' she retorted. 'But I've got to do better than you did. They didn't believe you, did they?'

That was true, of course. He resumed eating. After the first few mouthfuls he'd discovered that he was as hungry as a bear.

A waiter brought her tea and MacDonald watched as she sipped it. She smiled. 'Grandfather,' she said. 'Of course. I'll go and telephone him.' She rose as though her thoughts were a prelude to action. 'Excuse me. I'll meet you out on the verandah.'

He watched her cross the room, and only when it occurred to him that only a few diners were still around did he look at his watch. It was past nine o'clock! Up at the development, foremen would be wondering what had become of him, and this was the morning after the first real disaster.

He gulped down a few more mouthfuls and legged it out to the public telephones where Patricia had gone. She was not out there, which rather puzzled him. She'd hardly had

112

time to make the call down to Brentwood, let alone talk to her grandfather. He shrugged and stepped up to place his own call.

Then he remembered that the office was locked, so even though his foremen might hear the telephone ringing inside, they could not reach it. With a heartfelt curse he crossed the lobby and walked out on to the verandah.

She was waiting, and nearby was a battered jeep, muddy, dented, obviously from the Tolman Development Company's site up the mountain. He pointed to it.

She shrugged. 'I asked one of the men to bring it down when I came out earlier this morning.' As though that were a very natural thing, she brushed it aside and said, 'Grandfather is still not taking calls. You don't suppose he really *did* have a heart attack, do you?'

MacDonald, remembering his cynicism about this, winced. 'I hope not—for more reasons than one.' He glanced at the clear sky, at the fresh-washed distances, then over at her. 'How the hell do people get into these messes?'

She started down towards the car. 'By being obstinate, and opinionated, and overbearing, Mister MacDonald. But standing around down here isn't going to help, is it? At least we can go up to the development and see what damage was done and what corrective measures have to be undertaken.'

She climbed in on the passenger's side and waited for him to slide under the steering-wheel beside her. As he did this he shot her a look, saw the hard set of her jaw, the flattened position of her mouth, and sighed, quite overlooking the fact that she had just hurled an unpleasant remark at him.

'I'm sorry,' he said, starting the car and engaging the gears to drive out of the muddy yard and towards the uphill road. 'It just never occurred to me your parents might walk in. Or what they'd think if they walked in.'

She turned very slowly to consider his expression, then she reached impulsively and patted his arm. 'It's all right. I don't think I've been irredeemably compromised. No one is, any more, whether my parents belong to the stuffy generation or not. And anyway, even if I were, you are perfectly safe because if you were the last man on earth, I wouldn't marry you to save my reputation.'

He looked swiftly at her to see if she was joking. Evidently she was not because she wasn't smiling. He said, 'Well, that's just great. I couldn't imagine being married to a—a . . .'

'Yes, Mister MacDonald—a what?'

'Forget it,' he snarled, and set the car to the hill as though they were being pursued by the Mafia.

CHAPTER THIRTEEN

A DAY WITHOUT CRISES

When they arrived at the development she ran inside to answer a jangling telephone while he was intercepted by that same road-foreman who only the day before had been so demoralized over a little seam of water, and who today, in the face of a dozen washouts, looked self-satisfied. He gave MacDonald a report of damage as though he were reciting his catechism, ticking off each accounting on his fingers. When he was finished he said, evidently anticipating MacDonald's question, that he had divided his work crews so that at least two or three men were allocated to each damaged area.

MacDonald nodded. 'What is your estimate of when the messes will be cleaned up, and we'll be back on schedule?'

'Two, three days, providing I can have a couple of the bulldozers for the backing and filling.'

'You'll have them,' exclaimed MacDonald. 'I'll go and call them right away.' He strode off towards the office, without heeding the tangy forest-scent after the rain, or noticing that the air was free of dust, the visibility enormously improved.

Two or three days to recover from what he'd felt would amount to a minor calamity was not bad. Not bad at all. As he stepped inside and heard Patricia on the telephone in his office, he smiled a little, gratified and relieved. She completed her call, walked out where he was standing, and said, 'That was Grandfather's accounting firm down in Los Angeles. They heard the reports on the morning newscasts about a flash-flood up here and wanted to know the extent of damages.'

He was mildly annoyed. 'Don't even give us a chance to assess them. What did you say?'

She smiled. 'Just that. In a different way of course.'

'Of course.'

'I said if they were as prompt at delivering their monthly financial analysis to my Grandfather as they were about sticking their noses into other people's business, my Grandfather would be the best-informed investor in Southern California.'

'You didn't,' said MacDonald, shocked.

She kept smiling. 'I did.'

He fished round for his pipe, for the damp tobacco, and slowly smiled at her. 'Good for you. Well, I suppose I'd better get up to the disaster-area.' He tamped the pipe slowly. 'I don't suppose you'd care to ride along and see the damage?'

'Hadn't I better remain here and mind the store?'

He nodded, digging in his pockets for matches, which he did not find. She watched, and finally said, in her sweetest voice, 'If you're out of matches, perhaps now would be a good time for you to quit.'

In matching tones but without the smile he answered back. 'If you want to preach about the evils of tobacco I'll ask one of the carpenters to make you a soap-box.'

She nodded, properly rebuked. 'You're right. It's none of my business, is it?'

He didn't answer as he gave up the search for matches. 'I'll be back in an hour or two.' They stood looking at one another in the silent office, then he turned and walked outside.

She went as far as the door to watch him drive off. He had the un-lit pipe clamped between his teeth, which made her smile. He was not only a very independent male, he was also a stubborn one. Well, she'd already known how bull-headed he could be, so perhaps his independence shouldn't surprise her either.

She turned back as the telephone began ringing again. It promised to be an interesting, and hectic, day.

She did not see him again until past noon but nothing came up she did not feel qualified to handle, one way or another; things requiring his personal decisions she condensed in notes, and left them on his desk. Salesmen, men looking for work, estate agents interested in the progress of the development, she handled with tact.

In fact, she was in the midst of such a conversation when the mail arrived, brought up by the rural postman, and by the time she'd finished the conversation she had also sorted the letters into two piles. There was one letter left over. It was addressed to her in a variety of script she recognized quite well. In her Grandfather's youth very elegant handwriting had been a mark of distinction.

She opened the envelope with a feeling of scepticism. He began by saying he'd meant to get back up as he'd promised, but that he'd been prostrated, as she'd probably heard, by a heart ailment, minor of course, and she was under no circumstances to worry. He would be up and around in no time at all, then he would either drive up or have himself driven up, despite the fact that high altitude was most certainly going to be detrimental to his condition.

If she'd ever had doubts, she lost them now. To the letter in her hand she said, 'You old fraud.'

He asked about Joseph MacDonald, about the development, about the progress being made, and if she had managed to overcome MacDonald's aversions, which she obviously had or otherwise she'd have at least called him.

She put the letter down, considered the telephone for a long time, then shrugged and resumed reading. Her grandfather also said he wanted her opinion on whether MacDonald should be retained after the sub-dividing had been completed, and perhaps put in charge of sales and promotion.

When she'd finished the letter she leaned back at the desk and speculated on the reason her grandfather had written more about MacDonald than he'd written about his million-dollar investment.

As if she didn't know!

Voices in the outer office caught her attention. One belonged to a complaining foreman, she could tell that just from the tone. The other voice belonged to MacDonald. She sighed, put the letter in a drawer and rose to take the rest of the mail into MacDonald's private office.

Later, having got rid of the foreman, MacDonald sang out for her, and when she entered his office he said, 'I never found out—can you type letters?'

'Yes.'

'Well,' he waved at the opened letters on the desk, 'Some of this junk has to he answered.' He looked up. 'Do you mind?'

'Not at all, I'd be glad to. Incidentally, I received a note from Grandfather Tolman.'

He considered her face, then gestured for her to be seated on the chair in front of his desk. 'Did he fire me too?'

'Not yet. My parents won't see him until this

evening. He asked about you. About whether you might consider heading up the sales and promotional end of things after the development is finished.'

He answered swiftly, as though she hadn't taken him by surprise at all. 'I don't know. Let's cross that bridge when we come to it.' He leaned forward gazing at her. 'What else?'

'Nothing very important. He said he'll try to get up here as soon as he can. He also said the altitude will no doubt nearly kill him, the implication being that if we insist on his visit his death will be on our hands.'

MacDonald smiled slowly, then he laughed and threw himself back in the desk-chair. 'Why does he act like this? Apart from saddling me with you he hasn't done anything so terrible has he?'

She coloured slightly. 'Maybe he feels saddling you with me is enough. Shall we get on with the letters?'

'Yeah, in a minute.' He cleared his throat. 'I was thinking on the drive back—maybe we ought to have dinner together tonight.'

'What brought that on?'

'Well. Your folks will reach the estate by tonight. They'll have seen your grandfather. If there's to be any furore it should happen about then, shouldn't it?'

'And you mean to be gallant. My defender?'

He started to blush. His lips flattened slightly as the air around them thickened with antagonism. She saw the rebuke coming and headed it off by speaking first.

'You are probably right. And thanks for the invitation, I'd love to have dinner with you.' She topped it off with a sweet smile, and that left him hanging up there ready to he unpleasant with no one to be unpleasant to.

He came down gradually, picking up one of the letters requiring an answer and began dictating.

For more than an hour they were employer and employee, and she returned to the other office to type the drafts of the letters when two straw-bosses arrived to say that the drainage systems had all worked very well carrying the run-off storm-water, and that clean-up crews were well along towards piling debris for burning.

She could hear the three of them casually talking in MacDonald's office very easily. No one ever seemed to close a door in the log building. No one did so now.

Finally, one of the men mentioned her, it was along towards the tag-end of that impromptu conference, and his words sounded casual.

'I got to hand it to you, Mac. That Tolman girl don't look like she'd be able to shape things up, but she's pretty damned good.'

There was a pause. She could visualize MacDonald's gaze drifting to the open door because he knew she was within hearing.

Before he could check the foreman, if that had been his intention, the man spoke again.

'How many pretty gals do you know that could scrounge up wheel-lugs on short notice and talk me out of a man to put them in your car, on a busy day like today?' The foreman's chuckle was warm. 'Your car's as good as new.'

The pause came again. Patricia, beginning to wince in anticipation of MacDonald's roar, held both hands poised above the typewriter waiting for the thunder and lightning. All that happened was that MacDonald quietly said, 'Yeah. Well, she surprised me too. This isn't exactly downtown Los Angeles, up here.'

The men laughed together, then she heard their chairs scrape and a moment later heard their booted feet tramp out into the forward office near the front door. More was said, but she could only make out the low sound of masculine voices. Furiously, she went back to work on the letters, but she also kept one eye cocked towards the doorway expecting him to loom up, over there.

He did not appear. An hour later, at quitting time, she knew he was out front on the verandah going through the daily routine of accepting final judgements as foremen and workmen came in from the working areas to the car-park.

A half-hour later, she finished the last letter, listened to the silence that always arrived when the last workman had headed

122

down the hill towards Crestline, and took the letters to his office where she left them arranged for signing. Then, because he was not in the office and the front door was open towards the forest, she stepped out there and looked around.

He was seated nearby, feet up, beer can in hand, smoking. 'Come on out,' he said. 'This is the best time of day.'

She obeyed, mentioned the letters being ready, and watched as his pensive glance drifted up to her. He said, 'Thanks for taking care of the car for me. I didn't know that was part of a secretary's work.'

'How did you expect to get down to the village this evening, otherwise?'

'Hadn't thought much about it. Take one of the company cars, I suppose.' He removed the pipe and said, 'Of course you heard what that straw-boss said this afternoon, in my office.'

She nodded. 'They talk like men using foghorns. I couldn't have avoided hearing.'

'Yeah,' he muttered, and got to his feet. 'I hate to flatter people. It goes to their head.'

'If you're referring to me, Mister MacDonald, forget it. It doesn't go to my head, but I don't need it anyway. As for the car—the idea of a secretary is to try and keep as much detail off the boss's shoulders as possible. If you don't need that done, then all you need is a stenographer, or someone to answer the telephone.'

123

He listened, nodded thoughtfully, then smiled. 'Okay. Shall we stand here until one of us gets mad and starts an argument, or shall we get our sweaters and ride back down to civilization—such as it is?'

'I vote for civilization,' she said, and laughed at him as she went back inside to get her handbag and sweater. If there had ever been a crisis, obviously it had passed, at least as far as her taking the initiative in having his car fixed, was concerned.

CHAPTER FOURTEEN

A BIRTHDAY?

Things at the lodge were under control again. The manager, seeing MacDonald and Patricia Tolman enter, threw them a wave. Loud voices coming from the Redwood Room indicated that the construction workers were having their usual pre-dinner drink before trooping out to wash and clean up.

MacDonald halted at the base of the stairs and waved her on up, then he turned as the manager approached.

'You had a call a few minutes ago,' exclaimed the manager. 'It was from Brentwood. I told them to try in an hour, that you hadn't come in yet.'

124

Mac nodded sombrely. 'Did they leave a name?'

'No. Just said they'd try later and hung up.'

Mac said, 'Thanks,' and turned to head up to his room for a shower and a change. Evidently the Tolman Juniors had got home, and had spoken with Tolman Senior. If the outcome of this meant that someone had called to confirm that MacDonald had been fired, he was prepared for it.

What he did *not* like was the implication directed towards Patricia. By the time he'd finished showering, changing, and was ready to head down for the dining room, he had come to a decision: If that person in Brentwood called back, and if they mentioned Patricia in any way that was not to her credit, MacDonald was going to lower a verbal boom on them. Construction engineers knew words and expressions that would curl the hair of the ordinary John and Jane.

Patricia was already in the lobby when he arrived, with two shiny-faced and eager-eyed young men from the development smilingly overwhelming her with their charm. As unsmiling MacDonald walked up, the young men made a couple of feeble jokes, saw not even a flicker of appreciation in MacDonald's eyes, and excused themselves. Mac then asked if Patricia would care to have a drink in the Redwood Room, or at their dining table. She opted for the dining table, and rose for him to escort her.

She smelled bewitchingly of that scented soap, and her dinner dress was a shade of powder blue that matched her eyes. She obviously had dressed carefully, so he said, 'You look very handsome tonight, Miss Tolman.'

All he got for that gallantry was a slow, long look and not a word.

Their table near the window overlooking the rear garden had fresh linen and even a delicate sculptured vase with one magnificent yellow rose in it. He looked soberly at the rose. 'Whose birthday?' he asked, holding her chair then going round to seat himself. He missed the quick stabbing look of exasperation she shot at him. 'I'm in a mood for rare roast beef tonight,' he exclaimed. 'How about you?'

'If you're going to have a heavy meal, I think I'll just have a salad and some tea.' She said it almost spitefully.

He settled the napkin before glancing over at her. 'Now what have I done?'

'It's no one's birthday, and *I* had that rose put there!'

'Oh. Well—I didn't mean anything. They've never put flowers on my table before. It's a very pretty rose, isn't it?'

The waiter came, took their orders and departed. The last thing, just before he left, Patricia picked up the vase and held it out for the waiter to take with him.

MacDonald considered the shiny window. When the bar-steward arrived he ordered Scotch and soda. Patricia ordered a gin collins. Their eyes met, held briefly, then MacDonald mentioned the telephone call from Brentwood, which had the effect of making her forget the yellow rose.

'My father?'

'I don't know,' he replied. 'They left no name. Probably was, though, and I'm probably fired.'

'Then we are *both* fired.'

He turned that over in his mind. 'No; it's a bad thing to have serious disagreements in a family. You can just take over for the next engineer on the job. Anyway, things are about wound up.' He smiled. 'You could probably do what has to be done by yourself, without any engineer, from here on.'

'No, thank you.'

Their drinks arrived and beyond the window shadows floated inward and downward from the uphill forest. The moon, which had had difficulties being seen the night before, was up there tonight, three-quarters full and seemingly close enough to reach forth and touch.

'I'm curious about something,' he said eventually, sitting relaxed and with one hand holding his highball glass. He was looking at her with a critical and interested expression. 'Why did you say, this morning, that you wouldn't marry me if I were the last man on earth?'

'You haven't asked me to, have you?'

He was thrown for a small toss by her rejoinder. It was not what he'd expected. She saw his condition and followed it up quickly.

'And you aren't going to ask me, are you? But that wouldn't be the entire reason, Mister MacDonald. The rest of it would be because you are just naturally overbearing and disagreeable.'

His grip on the highball glass tightened. 'It couldn't possibly be that you, Miss Tolman, are too spoilt and . . .' He suddenly clamped his jaws closed. For about five seconds he sat like that, looking as grim as death. Then he turned loose all over, lifted his highball glass and said in a totally altered voice, 'To your smile, Miss Tolman. There isn't another one like it in the world.'

He drank and put the glass down as she did not even move. The spell was broken when the waiter arrived with their food, his platter of roast beef, her elegantly arranged but hardly very filling, salad and tea.

She seemed suspended between moods and he may have realized this, or he may have enjoyed throwing her off balance. Then again, since he dived into his meal, he may simply have chosen to let the silence between them drift onward because he was hungry.

The lodge-manager came over and handed

him a note, smiled benignly at them both and departed. He looked after the man with annoyance, read the note and passed it over to her. It was a telephone message saying that the following morning some inspectors from the State Realty Commission would arrive to see how the development had weathered the storm.

'But everything will be cleaned up by then,' she exclaimed.

He shrugged and returned to his meal. 'Did you expect *intelligent* action from bureaucrats, Miss Tolman?'

'You sound just like my grandfather.'

He reached for his cup of coffee. 'Why limit it just to us? Wait. You'll see these mini-minds in the morning. Afterwards, if you'd like, you can include yourself.'

She finished eating first but he wasn't very far behind. She produced something from a pocket and laid it in front of his plate. He began filling his pipe as she did this, and looked down at the round metal object with a faint scowl of curiosity.

'What is it?'

She said, 'After the rose episode I've been arguing with myself whether to give it to you or not. Try it.'

He picked the round object up, slid back what appeared to be a hexagonal collar in the middle of it, and at once a bright, white flame shot downward. 'Pipe-lighter,' he said. 'I'll be damned.' He smiled at her.

'I know,' she said quickly. 'It's not your birthday. But I don't want to have to carry matches for you, and that ought to absolve me.'

'Well, thank you, Miss Tolman.' He tried the lighter and it worked very well. 'Thank you very much. I'm speechless.'

'It must be the first time in your life.'

He puffed. 'Now listen, don't start an argument.'

She came near to smiling at him as she rose. 'Yes, master. I mean—no, master, I won't start an argument.'

He also rose. 'Could we go out on to the verandah for a bit?' he asked. 'Or would you like a drink in the bar or something?'

'The verandah will do just fine, Mister MacDonald.'

She led the way. Men looked up as they picked their way out of the dining-room and across the large lobby. There were also a few women, mostly guests of the lodge, holidaymakers, although not very many, who followed their progress across the rooms and out into the pleasant moonlit night.

He asked if she'd like his jacket, but it wasn't really cold. Crisp, but not cold. She went to the far railing up towards the darkened southerly end of the verandah, leaned there looking out at the stiff-topped forest where it cast darkness in spiked array against the paler sky, and took down a deep breath. When she turned he was watching her. She said, 'Look, it really isn't anything. I saw it in a store and bought it. You needed something like it. Don't get all wishy-washy over a functional thing like a pipe-lighter.'

'Miss Tolman, I am *not* getting wishy-washy.'

'Well. You *look* like you are . . .'

He continued to stand there facing her, his broad back and shoulders obstructing her view of the long porch, back towards the front entrance, and beyond. He reached for her as naturally as though he had every right, and she responded in the same manner, allowing herself to be drawn forward two steps. He removed the pipe and bent his head. She came still closer, slightly, and raised her head. It was the most natural kiss in the world.

Afterwards she said, 'It was easy, wasn't it, Mister MacDonald?'

'No. It was accidental. Well—sort of accidental.' He put his pipe aside and laid both hands upon her waist. 'And it wasn't by way of thanks for the lighter. But this one is.'

That time the kiss was different. She felt his strength and his desire, and moved her lips under the pressure but could not escape, and didn't really want to escape.

With raised arms upon his shoulders she held him for as long as the kiss lasted, then pushed him away and stepped back to the railing again. That time neither of them made an analysis. It would have been too embarrassing. Both had scared the other with a need and a hunger.

She let her breath out slowly. 'The telephone should ring—or something—right this minute, Mister MacDonald.'

He smiled gently. 'Or something, Pat. Don't you suppose that Mister MacDonald stuff could sort of get lost, now? When you've been kissed by a man, and still call him Mister, doesn't that make him seem like an uncle?'

'Yes, I suppose so. But I don't know exactly what I feel right at this minute. You realize we're not very compatible, don't you? Then what's the point?'

'How do you know we're not compatible?'

She looked squarely up into his face. 'What a thing to say! We've fought like dog and cat ever since . . .'

'Wait a minute. How would *you* have reacted if *I'd* arrived here with my rich grandfather to just take over the running of the office without a word of encouragement? It wasn't incompatibility—it was indignation. Something like that.' He faltered, looking round for the pipe, found it and held it in both hands to have something to do while he organized his thoughts to go on speaking. 'Are you implying that there was no point in me kissing you?'

She looked away for a second, then back.

'I'm really not up to arguing right at the moment—Mac. Or do you prefer Joe?'

'Mac is fine.'

'Oh, would it be all right if we didn't argue until tomorrow? I've got some thoughts to unravel and sort out.'

He reached, took her hand and held it gently. 'Sure.' They smiled at each other. 'Who wants to argue anyway?' he said, and turned to lead her slowly back towards the doors. 'It's late and if you didn't sleep any better than I did last night you'll be tired.'

He took her all the way back to the doorway, and on through to the foot of the stairs where he said, 'Goodnight. See you at breakfast,' and as she turned to hike on up, he went in search of the lodge-manager.

'Frank, I want a yellow rose in a vase sent up to her room. To Miss Tolman's room, I meant to say.'

'Sure, Mac. That's where I'd have sent it anyway.'

'And tell me something, Frank. What kind of a gift would she like?'

'Gift? Is it her birthday?'

'Damn it, does it always have to be someone's birthday?'

'No. No, of course not. Well, let me see. Why don't you. . . . Listen, Mac, let me go and ask my wife and report back. Okay?'

'Fine. I'll be in the bar.'

CHAPTER FIFTEEN

BIG TROUBLE

She rode to the development office with him the following morning after breakfast, and she seemed more preoccupied than usual, which wasn't strange at all. She even forgot to ask if the person calling from Brentwood had called back for him. They hadn't, and Mac forgot too or he'd have told her they hadn't.

The only variation in the morning routine occurred an hour after everything had been organized for the day, when two well-fed men driving a dark car with the Great Seal of the State of California on the door, arrived. They were from the Realty Commission, they told Patricia, and were scheduled to look the development over after the storm of two nights earlier.

Mac was over in the lakeside plot smoothing out some surveying and power-line difficulties. She said the inspectors could either look around without Mister MacDonald, or if they'd prefer she would try to contact him on the inter-communication system and ask him to return to the office.

The inspectors said they could do what had to be done without any help, and departed. Pat immediately called over to the lakeside area and asked that the word be passed to Mac that the Realty Commission inspectors had arrived and were doing whatever Realty Commission inspectors got paid to do.

When the second car drove up out front and the large, well-dressed man climbed out and stood gazing around for a moment, she watched the inspectors nod as they passed the newcomer on their way to their State car. She also speculated on the business of the large, well dressed newcomer. He let her speculate as he made a deliberate study of the forest, of the roads leading off through groves of huge trees, and finally, when he faced fully around, while he examined the log office building. Finally, he walked on up to the porch and inside. When he saw Patricia he removed his hat to reveal immaculate grey hair. He smiled at her.

'You are Miss Tolman?'

She nodded.

'I'm George Merriman, Miss Tolman, construction engineer connected with Blevins, Given and Merriman in West Los Angeles.' He offered her a calling card and kept studying her rather closely as he spoke. 'It was suggested to my firm that perhaps we ought to have someone drop by up here and look things over.'

Pat, with a premonition, put Mister Merriman's card upon a map-table and looked directly at him. 'For what reason, Mister

Merriman?'

His smile was paternal. 'Well, for this trip at any rate, as a sort of consultant.'

'We don't need a consultant, Mister Merriman. And we have a licensed engineer on the job.'

'Yes. So I was told, Miss Tolman.' Merriman turned away from her and stood gazing out of a front window. 'Beautiful spot up here, isn't it? Obviously it'll be a winner. A money-maker for your father.'

'For my *grand*father.'

Merriman turned with a cocked brow. 'I was under the impression your grandfather was out of it.'

Patricia moved slowly round behind the dividing counter of the outer office and leaned there gazing at the large, grey, and well-groomed older man. 'Where would you get such an impression, Mister Merriman?'

He smiled and said nothing as they looked at one another. Obviously, he was not going to be drawn into a conversation. Patricia seethed. She thought she knew what was happening. With a flourish she whirled and went to the rearmost office, which she had taken over. From there she put in a transceiver call to the lakeside area for Mac. When he came on she said, 'I think you'd better come back here on the double. We have a very elegant and smiling engineer walking around like he just might be someone's successor. Are you coming?'

136

'Be right back.'

She put the transceiver down, picked up the telephone and dialled her home down in Brentwood. The pulse in the side of her neck was beating strongly and there was a steely look to her glance.

First a servant answered, then her mother came to the telephone. Patricia was forthright in a pleasant way, but she didn't *look* very pleasant when she said, 'Mother, whose idea was it to send Mister Merriman up here?'

Elyse sounded agitated. She also looked it but of course her daughter could not discern that. 'Now, Patricia, your father and I simply had to make the final decision. It's been a long time coming, and we just couldn't side-step it any longer.'

'What decision, Mother? What are you talking about?'

'Your grandfather deliberately sent you up there into that—that *environment*. We faced him squarely on the issue as soon as he got back home last evening, and he had the gall to confirm our worst suspicions. Not only that, but he was terrible to us both. So your father contacted that engineering establishment—he knew one of the partners, you see—it's an eastern company with headquarters in—'

'Mother! I don't care a damn where their headquarters are! One of them is up here this morning. In fact, he's in the outer office right this minute. What is he supposed to do,

137

replace Joseph MacDonald?'

'Yes, child. You see, your father and I—'

'What about *Grandfather*? Is he really ill, Mother? Is that why you're doing this?'

'Patricia, you know what he did. By now you've surely figured it out. Horrid person. He fooled us all. He no more had a heart attack than I did.'

'Then how can you and Father take over like this?'

'Patricia, you're raising your voice to your mother!'

Pat sank down behind her desk, rocked far back in the swivel-chair, then said, eyes on the knotty-pine ceiling. 'Sorry, love. It's just, you see, that you've got my insides all tied in a knot.'

'Patricia! You see what that environment is doing to you? You're even beginning to *talk* like those—men up there.'

'Mother! The first time I heard that was at the University, *not* here at the development! Now let's get back to facts. How can you and Dad take over like this? You are not even involved in the development, are you?'

'Your father, *Patricia*, is guardian and protector of your grandfather.'

'Mother, if this wasn't so tragic I'd die laughing. Dad, God love him, is no one's protector. Not mine and not Grandfather's. Maybe he's your protector, but that's all. Are you actually telling me he's trying to have

138

Grandfather declared incompetent or something like that?'

'Patricia, your father and I will drive up tomorrow to bring you home. If your father believes any of this concerns you, he'll discuss it with you at that time. Anyway, love, I don't understand all he told me this morning.'

'Mother, let me speak to Grandfather.'

'He's not here, child.'

Patricia rocked slowly forward to lean on the desk. She was totally unaware of two masculine voices in the far, outer office. She couldn't have heard them anyway, except as a low growl of distant sound.

'Where is he, Mother?'

'I frankly don't know, Patricia. He and your father had words this morning right after breakfast. I left. It was the worst argument I've ever heard. Then your grandfather slammed out of the house, got into his car and drove away.'

'I see; and Father called in his attorneys. Mother, if you and Dad want to drive up here tomorrow, that's fine with me, but I probably won't be going back with you, and you might as well know right now—both of you—that since you are set on making a mountain out of a molehill, I'm going to take the side of Grandfather—*and* Joe MacDonald.'

She put the telephone back upon its stand with an angry gesture, then slumped against the desk gazing out through the office doorway to a window a dozen or so feet beyond. Outside, the sun was shining, birds were singing, giant pines stood as they'd been standing a hundred and more years, and only inside, in her office, was the world all topsy-turvy.

'Hullo. You look like you have inside information about the end of the world.'

He leaned in the doorway, grinning, big and bronzed and self-assured. She propped her head on both fists. 'I did a very dumb thing. I should have telephoned my parents last night the moment they got back home, and explained.'

'What have they done—besides sending Merriman up here?'

'Isn't that enough?'

'No. My deal is with the *senior* Tolman. That's what I told Merriman. If he comes back tomorrow with an order from your *grand*father for me to pack up and move on, I'll do it. But that's the only way.'

'They are coming up tomorrow to take me back home.'

'Are you going, Pat?'

'No! Of course I'm not going!'

He grinned wider. 'Nothing to be so upset about. How old are you?'

'Almost twenty-three.'

'You see? Like I said, there's no cause for alarm. You are of age and can do as you jolly well damned please. Go back or stay here.' He eased forward, sought a chair and sank down into it. 'Can you get your grandfather on the telephone?'

'No. He walked out of the house. They had a big fight, or something and he left.'

Mac drummed on the arm of the chair, eyes slitted. 'That's not too good, is it? We'll need his support, I suppose.' He leaned suddenly and held forth his large palm for her to lay her hand upon. When she did that he closed his fingers. 'What you need is the afternoon off. Have you ever been in the back-country hereabouts?' She did not answer. He rose, still holding her fingers, pulling her up with him. 'Come along. We'll both take the afternoon off. As for the disturbances down home, let's forget it for a while.'

She allowed him to lead her out of the office and down towards the front of the building where the reception-room was, before she freed her hand and said, 'This isn't going to help a bit, Mac. Running never does.'

He laughed quietly. 'We're not running. No one who only takes one half of one day off from work is running. We're just going to kick ourselves free of some temporary unpleasantness, then come back later this evening feeling fresh enough to face it. Coming, Pat?'

She nodded. 'But I'm not going to be very good company, Mac. It makes me feel miserable. My parents brawling with

Grandfather. And all because I did something they misinterpreted.'

'That's the point, Pat. I suppose parents have a right to mistrust their kids, and no doubt about it, if I'd been in your dad's shoes I'd probably have thought, and reacted, about the same way he did. But the point is—you are of age, you didn't do anything wrong, and it's up to them to listen to you; to give you a chance to have your say as an adult as well as a daughter.'

He took her out on to the front porch where sunlight striking irregularly downward from high treetops gave the office, the surrounding solitude, the quiet yard and segment of roadway, a cathedral softness.

'Do you know anything about Indians?' he asked.

She let him steer her towards his car. 'Indians? Well, I know they didn't like General Custer.'

He laughed and held the door for her. 'I'm going to show you some pictographs they painted on the lee-side of some rocks— nobody knows how long ago. And some caves on the Bakersfield side of the Grapevine where they lived a half a millenia ago. I even know where there is a soda-spring up here, and a pool of spring-water clear as glass and warm enough to swim in.'

He backed clear and drove slowly out of the forest to the roadway. The sun was almost

142

directly overhead. He said they would stop first down at the village for lunch, before starting their adventures. By the time they were halfway down the hill she was beginning to feel better although not a single one of her problems had been resolved, nor for the matter of that, even thought through.

She knew, for example, that before she faced her parents the following day, she had to talk to her grandfather. And at present that possibility seemed about as remote as the moon because she had no idea where he would go storming off to when he was angry.

CHAPTER SIXTEEN

TANGLED EMOTIONS

Of course, having been in the area longer, it was possible MacDonald would know something about it. She had never asked many personal questions and she did not ask any now, when he took a side-road off the main expressway, but that did not prevent her from wondering when he'd ever found the time to go exploring.

The road he now followed eventually turned to ruts filled with pine needles. It was not very smooth but it was quite cool where the sun never reached, and very fragrant.

There was a rather large clearing, eventually, where he could turn the car completely around without effort, and here he switched it off, climbed out and beckoned for her to follow.

She had the feeling that if she didn't hasten after him she'd be lost. This particular part of the forest was dense and gloomy and confusing. She kept him well in sight despite his long stride.

They came to a much smaller clearing where sandstone slabs about five feet in height had either been brought here, or had been found here and had been raised into an upright position, then packed round the base with dirt that over the centuries had turned nearly as hard as the sandstone. There were four such slabs. Each one was decorated, but where MacDonald led Patricia, behind the broadest of those stones, was a discernible, although fast-fading painting of a man, head back, arms up and outflung, evidently praying, or calling upon the Great Spirit. The art was crude but the force of the effigy's pleading stance came through with simple power.

MacDonald said, 'Does he ask for game, perhaps?'

She stood close beside MacDonald. 'No. For peace, I think, for protection.' She looked all around this tiny glade, lost for centuries, or if known, at least ignored and forgotten. 'When was the last Indian here, Mac?'

'Two, three hundred years ago I'd guess.'

'You see? His prayer wasn't answered, was it? His Great Spirit was looking in some other direction, listening to another prayer. He didn't protect them because they are gone.'

Mac looked from the dim painting to Patricia, then back to the stone again. With approval he said, 'Very good, remarkable, in fact. I can feel it that way now, myself.' He winked at her. 'You have a soul.' He took her hand and went deeper through the hushed, warm forest. Once, where a fire had cleared a bony ridge, they stopped to look over the shimmering distance of the San Joaquin Valley, the richest single valley in all North America.

Where they followed a game-trail downward to a shady creek, he showed her a soda-spring. The water tasted like coca-cola. Here, again, were slabs raised upright, but without decorations this time. He said, 'Health spa.'

She was interested and curious. 'Because of the water?'

He nodded. 'Drink enough of it and you'll find out.'

She did not press the subject. Anyway, he turned southward now and where a trail loomed, wider than the other trails. They hiked along for nearly an hour before he halted in mid-trail, pulled her around in front and with both hands on her shoulders, pointed her so that she faced a greeny opening through tall sentinel pines.

There was a still-water pool half a hundred yards ahead in a grassy glade. Several does with fawns were in the grass, wholly unsuspecting. A creek off to their right pushed through dark green saw-grass and ripgut coming from some distant, secret spring to feed the little pond. Its natural spillway was northward, down through a shallow arroyo towards the soda-spring.

He kept his hands on her shoulders as he said, 'Adam and Eve.'

'In the Garden,' she murmured, and smiled in the direction of the deer. 'What a delightful spot.'

'Care to go swimming?'

'I have no suit.'

'No matter, Eve. Neither have I.'

She stepped out from under his hands, the deer sighted movement, flung up their heads, then fled in a flash to the deeper shadows and disappeared. She walked slowly down to a glassy place where lily pads scarcely moved when astonished small frogs dived off them striving for the dark depths.

'What did they do here?' she asked, turning to look back at him. 'Bathe? Launder their clothes? Teach their children to swim?'

He smiled. 'Probably. And on full-moon nights they'd make love or sing, or maybe cook a stolen beef from some lowland ranch.' He knelt to test the water. It was cold without being terribly so. As he rose again to his full height he said, 'It was pretty simple, living life as it came. Too simple to last, I'm afraid.'

'What happened to them? They didn't all just die, did they?'

He stoked and lit his pipe. 'When I was a kid an old half-breed Indian woman who did our laundry in the Midwest told me one time what did the redskin in was the iron-pot.'

She frowned faintly.

He grinned at her. 'Not the rifle. They had rifles too. Not the number of settlers, because they had lots of land to retreat into and manoeuvre over. She said before the iron-pot her redskin-people cooked with heated stones dropped into reed baskets. It was pretty crude. Then they got the iron-pot. After that they couldn't go back to hot stones in reed baskets, so in order to buy iron-pots meaning all the other conveniences the whites brought they had to trap for the whites, work in the hayfields, learn trades and even, eventually, to dress like whites. You see the point?'

Pat saw it and said, 'Well; at least they didn't die or get massacred or something horrible.'

He shrugged.

The sun was dropping a little, the upper end of their glade was turning dusty. Crickets in damp places made their song and a very brave little wet-shiny frog at the farthest end of the pond sat on a lily pad and croaked defiance at the intruders.

She said she would return with her bathing suit one day, then she smiled at him. 'I'm glad I came, Mac.'

He led her back where forest-shade formed a barrier against the sun. There, they sat in short-cropped grass near several deer-beds with only silence and sunshine, shade, and restfulness for companions. He finished the smoke, knocked the pipe empty, stowed it and lay back, head cradled on both arms.

'I had an original thought last night, Pat. Would you care to hear it?'

He wasn't looking at her, he was gazing straight up through dark pine limbs to the dusty-rose sky, but she was a woman, with a woman's intuition, and they were alone in a private place in a kind of personal limbo, so she was careful with her answer.

'If it's a new problem I don't think we need it, do we?'

He rolled his head sideways, glanced at her thoughtfully, then rolled it away. 'Probably not.'

She felt vague disappointment. She also felt vague disapproval with herself. She leaned towards him slightly. 'I'm sorry. Of course I'd like to hear it. But even here it's not quite possible to forget those other things, is it?'

He contradicted her. 'It's easy for me. I guess to someone like you the end of the world is an unkind word.' He started to raise up as though the conversation, and the mood, was finished.

She reached to push him back down with a hand on the chest. 'Tell me your original thought, Mac. Please?'

He sat up despite her restraining hand, and looked at her with a grave face. 'Did you ever hear that song that says there is a time for planting and a time for reaping, a time for playing and a time for dying? Well, right now I think it's time to be heading back.' He shot upright and held out a hand to her, pulled her to her feet and smiled softly. 'For a little while you forgot, and that's what you needed. For a while there you were letting the world close in on you. That's never any good.' He tugged her forth out into the bright sunshine and towards the wide trail leading back out of the glade.

'You lead,' he told her. 'Let's see if you can find your way back without a guide.'

It was over. Whatever he'd thought of back in the pine-shade, was finished. She knew, the moment he took her back out into sunshine and away from the blessed shade.

She took the lead wordlessly and with unerring steps got back to the soda-spring. That was no hardship in any case because of the wide trail. But from the soda-spring back eastward towards the painted sandstone slabs she had to concentrate hard, had to keep seeking the tell-tale pressed-down grass, the crunched-over dry pine needles where his boots had borne down, and once, when he laughed because she was following a false trail, she got furiously angry with him but without letting it show.

Finally, they reached the painted slabs and she was relieved enough to look ruefully at him, and smile. 'As a Camp-Fire Girl I'd flunk the tenderfoot test.'

'You did very well. Considering.'

Her gaze flashed out at him. 'Considering what? That I'm a spoilt little rich girl who doesn't know up from down?'

He let her wrath break over him unmoved. 'No. What I meant was—considering that you've never been here before. Actually, my first time I got hopelessly lost, so you did better than I did.' He didn't give her a chance to show contrition. 'Okay, from here on I'll lead.' He stepped out in the final leg of their trek without looking at her again, or even speaking, until the car was in sight. Then he asked if she was thirsty and said he had a canteen in the back of the car.

She wasn't thirsty. She was miserable. But he got the canteen anyway, so she drank a little, then watched him drink. She had made a disaster out of what he had wanted to be pleasant for them both. For the next half hour she wouldn't even have bought herself on a slave block for two cents.

He reversed the car and headed back, then

he paused in a clearing to point out the streak of bloody sky over beyond the distant, westerly mountains. The sky looked real, even the egg-yolk sun looked real, but those tannish, cardboard mountains were as false as could be.

Swaying and pitching in wheel-ruts, he laughed and said, 'Funny thing about people. What's one person's meat is another person's rhubarb.'

She interpreted that to mean he thought she hadn't enjoyed the afternoon. 'It was lovely,' she exclaimed. 'It was like stepping back through time. Peaceful and beautiful, and so sad.'

He looked at her, but had to put his attention back upon the road where they came to the expressway again. An immense truck-tractor roared past dwarfing his car. It gave two hoots on an air-horn that bounced wildly back and forth through the mountains until its echoes were lost in the forest.

It was nearly seven o'clock. She was shocked. If she'd been asked to guess the time she'd have said four-thirty in the afternoon, or perhaps even less. When Crestline hove in sight, in its trough where sunlight vanished early, they could see cars out in front of the lodge, lighted windows all around the village, and definite night-time everywhere except upon the higher ridges, far away.

'Like something out of *Snow White and the Seven Dwarfs*,' he murmured, and grinned a little self-consciously. 'Hungry?'

She was—and she wasn't. 'A little.' She twisted on the seat. 'You could ask me to dinner again.'

'Fine.' He fished in a pocket, brought forth a small package and dropped it in her lap. They were close enough to the turn-off so he couldn't look away from driving. 'I'll meet you in the dining-room as before.'

He swung into his private parking space, killed the motor and climbed out, all in a couple of smooth movements. He seemed anxious to get away. 'Half an hour,' he said, and hiked off leaving her in the car looking after him. He hadn't even given her a chance to thank him for the afternoon.

The little box in her hand no doubt was the reason. He was not a man who liked being embarrassed, and if she'd opened the box, then had exuded pleasure, gratitude, appreciation, he'd have been embarrassed. For the first time in an hour she smiled. It didn't make everything right, but it helped.

She left the car and went hiking round to the front verandah where several loafing workmen watched her progress to the front door, where she disappeared. Then the workmen looked significantly at one another without a word being said.

CHAPTER SEVENTEEN

MARRY ME!

It was a cameo brooch. The setting was new gold and carefully wrought by a genuine craftsman. The cameo was darker than most she'd seen, with the girl's profile more perfectly carved. She was surprised because it was a very expensive gift, and also because, although the gold was new the stone looked very old, perhaps antique.

It was far too fine a present to give to someone who was simply an acquaintance or a friend. She showered and dressed very slowly, with the cameo on the dressing table in front of her, torn between emotions. She really shouldn't accept it, keep it, and unless he had some serious reason he shouldn't have given it to her.

Finally, having chosen a white linen dress with a bolero jacket and a creamy blouse because they complemented his gift, she fastened it in place above her right breast. It looked as though the dress had been made only to be worn with the brooch.

She went downstairs, saw by a lounge-clock that it was past eight o'clock, felt surprised again at the lateness, and headed for the dining-room.

He was already at their table. Also, that self-same little fluted glass vase was the centre-piece, and in it was a yellow rose. She suddenly remembered that she'd completely neglected to thank him for the one he'd sent her the night before. She was, she told herself a little frantically, making a mess of everything.

When he rose to hold her chair, though, she smiled as though she hadn't a nerve in her body. Then she said, 'Mac, it's so lovely I don't know what to say.' She teetered on the verge of reproaching him for extravagance, but remembering how she'd spoiled things earlier, she let that go and said instead, 'Did you look at it closely? The cameo is very old.'

He leaned to study the thing but a waiter interrupted and after they had ordered he simply said, 'There is another surprise for you, but I had nothing to do with it. Your grandfather is upstairs taking a nap.'

It *was* a surprise. 'My grandfather, here?'

'Yes. The manager told me when I came down for dinner. He arrived this afternoon, had lunch then said he didn't want to he disturbed and went up to take a nap.'

They sat looking at one another. Mac was amused by something but all Patricia could think of was the trouble they had so resolutely turned their backs on this afternoon, and how, as Mac had said, it was closing in on her from all sides.

He evidently mistook her anxious look

because he said, 'Don't worry, he's all right. I asked if he looked ill or anything. Frank said he looked fit as a fiddle and acted fine.'

'I suppose it's good he's here,' she murmured, and completely forgot the highball she'd meant to have before eating. 'But it's a surprise.'

'To you, maybe, not to me.' He did not elaborate on that perhaps because he did not mean to, or perhaps because as the waiter came with their dinner and he was hungry, it did not seem very important.

While they ate she had time to adjust to Grandfather Tolman's presence. She also had time to predict the outcome if her parents arrived the next day while Grandfather Tolman was still here. It seemed reasonable to encourage him to leave first, perhaps in the morning, early. But Grandfather Tolman was not a man who could be eased out of a situation unless he was ruddy well ready to depart.

'Don't look so worried,' said Mac, smiling across at her. 'I'm surprised you don't have ulcers.'

'How do you know I don't have? They'll make a scene if he's still here when my parents arrive tomorrow.'

'Good,' said Mac. 'I like scenes. It's like watching soap operas on television, only in three dimensions.'

'I don't think it's very funny, Mac.'

He put down his fork and straightened up. 'Learn to, Pat. Make a real effort to smile tomorrow when the bullets are flying thick and fast. When the trumpets are blowing.'

'You nut,' she growled, and finished her dinner. 'This happens to be a real family disaster.' She regarded him for a steady moment, then said, 'Tell me about your family. Didn't they ever have trouble?'

He turned this over in his mind, then shook his head. 'Not that I recall, although the day I bloodied the nose of a cousin visiting from Kansas City in the cow barn did upset my mother. My father, after hearing both sides, decided my cousin from Kansas City was a prig and when my mother got mad at him, he and I went to town, bought her a five-pound box of chocolates, and that evening the three of us sat around eating candy and discussing the possibility of late rains to help the wheat crop.'

She didn't believe him, but she smiled. 'You always catch me off-balance. And I don't believe you even had a cousin in Kansas City.'

He fished out his pipe, solemnly loaded it, fished out the jet-lighter, pushed back the middle section so the flint sparked and a darting tongue of flame erupted, and when he had a nice head of smoke up, he said, 'What good is a brooch anyway? Did you ever light a pipe with one?'

'Mac, be serious.'

He pocketed the lighter. 'Why? We'll be

156

serious all day tomorrow. Every day for ten to twelve hours I'm so serious my jaws get cramped. Not at night.' He let smoke drift away and turned to glance over the room. Almost as soon as he'd viewed the other diners he looked back towards her again. 'Care to try the verandah again tonight?'

He was bantering her. She nodded, put aside her napkin and rose. He let her precede him across the room and out into the large sitting-room. There was an enormous stone fireplace, large enough to take logs six feet long. Someone had lit it tonight, although the night of the thunderstorm, with chilly air coming off mountain snowfields, no one had bothered.

Outside, the three-quarters moon was fatter, more nearly round. It's brightness limned treetops and made the village glow softly. Cars and lorries passing out on the expressway made fire-fly trails with their headlamps behind which lurked darker shapes hastening to keep up and never quite making it.

She didn't go all the way down to the far, southern end of the verandah tonight, where it was dark and where he'd kissed her. She went only halfway along, and he halted not far from a lumpy deck-chair where someone sat mummy-like with a blanket over their feet and legs.

She turned abruptly. 'Mac, I know I spoiled

157

something for you up there at the pond today. I—I didn't really know how to answer. But I'm sorry for what I did.'

He puffed, leaned upon a peeled fir upright, hands in pockets, and considered her lovely face in moonlight. 'I think I like you better when you're angry,' he replied, rather drolly. 'I'm uncomfortable around contrite women.'

She returned his stare. 'I wish I could oblige but lately it's been getting harder for me to fly off the handle.'

'Worried?'

'It's not that—exactly,' she muttered, and turned away. She took down a fresh breath. 'The evenings up here are so beautiful this time of year.'

'My original thought, Patricia, was that you should marry me.'

She didn't move nor lower her head from contemplation of the moon-washed distant peaks that rose and fell, canted and leaned and flattened, as they ran off in all directions westerly and easterly. 'How is that original?' she asked quietly. 'People have been doing that for ten thousand years.'

'But *I* haven't, and *you* haven't.

'Anyway . . . we fight.'

'*You* fight. I'm the most even-tempered man in the world.'

'Even? Meaning mean *all* the time?'

'You're trying to start an argument, Pat.'

'You didn't want me around, remember?'

'That was long ago. Moreover, you can't possibly believe human relationships are forever static. Look; I'm in love with you. If it seems illogical to you, imagine how it seems to me.'

'What a queer proposal this is,' she said, and turned to face him without feeling any embarrassment or trepidation at all. 'And furthermore, Mac, I don't think you mean it.'

He knocked out his pipe with the calm deliberation of a warrior laying aside his shield to wield his sword with both hands. He pocketed the pipe and pulled straight up off the porch-support with about eighteen inches between them.

'Now you listen to me,' he said. 'One minute ago you were all tremulous over having cut me off short up at the pond. On the drive back this evening you were all slumped with self-abnegation. Now, when I tell you what it was I wanted to say, you're acting like some kind of super-sophisticate who refuses proposals of marriage every evening after supper. I *personally* think your parents neglected taking you over their knee often enough when you were a kid, but if—'

'I ought to belt you one,' she exploded at him, hauling straight up to her full height. 'I always knew you thought I was spoiled and—'

'Shut up! I'm not through speaking!'

'Don't you *dare* talk like that to me!' She whirled to step past. He caught her upper arm and whirled her back. She came half around, poised and hesitant, then she completed the turn and raised her arms to his shoulders. He swept her in close as though she were weightless. The lumpy figure on the nearby deck-chair, who had been witnessing all this, sat erect watching them embrace.

He heard her say something but it was too low to carry over even that small distance.

What she said was: 'Mac, take me back to the pond tomorrow.'

He kissed her a second time, then brushed her cheek as he nodded. 'First thing in the morning?'

'Yes. But—what about *them*?'

'Oh. How about just saying—to hell with *them*?'

'Mother worries, Mac.'

'Do you know what I think, sweetheart? She has a right to be worried—now.'

'Mac? Ask me again?'

'I didn't ask you before, I told you: You should marry me.'

'. . . All right.'

He pulled back, or tried to but she held his head down so he couldn't see her face. He asked if she meant it. She nodded and buried her face against his chest.

Moments later she worked free. 'You stay here until I've gone inside,' she told him, then she turned and walked rapidly away.

He did as she'd said, but faced forward so

he could see her go forward until she disappeared. Then he leaned against the upright-post again, shoved big fisted hands deep into trouser pockets, and very gradually became aware of a slight noise behind him, a short distance down the verandah. He recalled the lumpy deck-chair and didn't bother to turn. There had been witnesses; the verandah hadn't been entirely empty even when they'd first walked out on to it.

'Boy, come over here,' said a tinny voice from farther back. MacDonald's heart stood perfectly still for a second because he recognized that voice immediately. *Grandfather Tolman!*

He turned slowly, like a butterfly skewered to the upright-post. Grandfather Tolman was wearing a ridiculous checked cap, the gear—and prerogative—of college youths. The robe over his legs and feet was thrown back now as he beckoned.

MacDonald said, inanely, 'They said you were upstairs taking a nap.'

The old man puffed. 'How long do you think people work at taking naps? Come over and sit in this chair beside me. You know, that set-to rather reminded me of a couple of stray cats, a tom and a she-cat, getting acquainted. Now, no offence, you understand; maybe that's exactly what she's been needing. Only you don't take my granddaughter up to no pond in the woods tomorrow.'

161

MacDonald recovered from his surprise gradually, and strolled closer to the old man, but he did not sit in the chair, he simply stood gazing at the wizened man on the deck-chair. 'Look, Mister Tolman, if *she* wants to go, and if *I* want to take her, we'll just go. Maybe you other Tolmans haven't looked lately, but she's almost twenty-three years old. She quit being your little girl a long time ago.'

Grandfather Tolman's puckered eyes studied MacDonald's square-jawed features, then turned sly and amiable.

'Well, maybe. Tell me something, Mac. How did you happen to ask her to marry you tonight?'

'Why shouldn't I have asked her? If you heard that much you must have heard the rest of it.'

'I know. But only a couple of days ago you were going to quit just because she—'

'You're as bad as she is, Mister Tolman. Because something was one way a few days ago doesn't mean it always has to be that way, does it—dammit all!'

Grandfather Tolman held up a hand. 'Give me a tug up off this chair. Let's go to the bar and have a drink.'

CHAPTER EIGHTEEN

RETURN OF GRANDFATHER TOLMAN

Ordinarily a couple of drinks after dinner would make a man drowsy, but Grandfather Tolman's mind had been a vortex of thoughts before the drinks with MacDonald, so the stimulant worked differently on him; it hastened the thought-processes, and revitalized the physical ones.

After he'd heard about Mister Merriman and Pat's talk with her mother, Grandfather Tolman said, 'Well, Elyse has always tended to exaggerate. If that was the biggest argument she ever saw, why then she hasn't seen very many arguments. All *they* said was that I deliberately threw my granddaughter into this den of wolves up here only so that I could use her like I used everyone else for my own purposes. And I said the biggest mistake I ever made was in letting Davey's mother have the final word in raising him, because she'd turned out a nincompoop, a procrastinator, a pudgy-handed social parasite.'

MacDonald kept a perfectly straight face, but it was not easy. 'Bit hard on them, weren't you?'

'Nonsense,' snorted the old man. 'Anyway, by the time they got back to their wing of the house neither one of them remembered half of what I said.'

'I think you're underestimating them, Mister Tolman. Merriman—remember?'

'Pshaw! I don't know this Merriman, but that's ridiculous, saying they're taking over. I've got lawyers who'll laugh them out of the state if they try it.' Grandfather Tolman made an expansive gesture as though warding off flying insects. 'MacDonald, my son is my son. I'm a person with strong family feelings, but that don't mean I'm blind as a bat either. I know Davey's limitations better than he does—and that bird-brained wife of his—well—she loves Davey, and that's a rare thing.' Old Tolman smiled. 'You see? The Lord picked these relations of mine, I didn't. But I'm stuck with them, and maybe I wouldn't trade 'em for something smarter. But He sure pulled a stunner when he sent Davey and Elyse that baby I was so sure'd be a boy. And was Patricia. Only she turned out to have the spunk her parents don't have. You understand?'

'That she has spunk? Yes indeed.'

'No, damn it, not that she has spunk. Well, not *entirely* that. She's got brains and vision—*and* spunk.'

'Yes, sir, I agree.'

'And you're going to marry her.'

'Yes, sir.'

'Good.' Old Tolman had spoken his piece, had put things into proper perspective for them both, or so he thought, so he yawned, making a great show of hiding it, and afterwards, looking very apologetic, said, 'It's been a hell of a long day. *Couple* of days in fact. I think I'd better hit the hay.' He waggled a gnarled finger. 'When folks get up to my age, they just don't have the reserve they once had.' He rose, cocked a bright eye and said, 'I almost forgot. I drove up to the development this afternoon. Lucky I did. Wasn't no one around to lock the office. Not that it meant a whole lot. Anyway, I had a look around. Things are dandy, I got to hand it to you, Mac. Well, goodnight.'

Mac kept his eyes on the old man. 'I'd take it easy up those stairs if I were you, Mister Tolman. A man your age and all—and with a bad heart.'

'A bad . . . ? Oh yes, well as a matter of fact, Mac.'

'Yeah, I know, Mister Tolman. It was a fake attack.' MacDonald also rose from the bar, dropped some coins on to it, gave a wintry small smile and offered Tolman his arm. 'Feller gets into his eighties,' MacDonald said, mimicking Grandfather Tolman. 'He's got to expect a few things to go wrong. After all, he don't have much time left.'

Tolman's slitted eyes showed no appreciation nor humour. 'If I was forty years younger I'd whip you to a frazzle,' he growled.

Mac took hold of his arm and held firmly

when he would have squirmed free. As they went towards the door out of the bar the younger man said, 'Mister Tolman, everyone has their gimmick. Yours is the "pitiful-old-man" routine. It's all right with me. I don't judge people, I just watch them and maybe laugh a little.'

'Well, and what's your gimmick, then?' demanded Tolman, finally breaking free of MacDonald's grip.

'Well, up until a couple of days ago it's been my work. Since then it's been your granddaughter. If I could combine the two I think I'd have a pretty nearly invincible career.' He escorted Tolman to the foot of the stairs and faced him over there with a smile. He also shoved out a big hand. 'Do me a favour, will you, Mister Tolman?'

The older man gripped the extended hand, pumped it, hard, once, then dropped it. 'Sure. Name it.'

'Don't interfere.'

Old Tolman was not fooled by the mildness of MacDonald's voice or expression. 'It's m'nature, son, but I'll try not to.'

'What about tomorrow when your son and his wife drive in?'

'Don't worry about it, Mac. I'll make peace with them—the pair of ninnies.' He winked. 'Otherwise I won't interfere. We got a deal, eh?' He winked again then went marching up the stairs with a springy step, either neglecting

166

to consider his quavery heart or forgetting he had one.

Mac watched, then shook his head. 'That damned old devil is incorrigible,' he told himself aloud, and turned to go back to the bar for a nightcap.

Grandfather Tolman reached the second-floor landing and didn't hesitate to catch his breath but walked steadily along until he came to his granddaughter's rooms. There, he knocked lightly, then harder, until she called forth, then he identified himself and was admitted.

She had her hair held back from her face, which was shiny from scrubbing, and she was dressed in a functional but quite expensive quilted, satin robe. She had little gold-laced satin slippers to match. Instead of twenty-three she looked eighteen and her grandfather approved.

'I guess you didn't know that was me out on the verandah in the deck-chair, did you?' He laughed at the look of embarrassment she gave him. 'It's all right. Only I think you over-acted. He's a fine young man and—'

'Don't lecture me, Grandfather,' she said, beginning to look slightly hostile. 'You said you wanted me to keep an eye on the family interests up here; to represent you and a lot of other bunk. I know why you put me up here!'

'You do?' he asked, feigning incredulity.

'Joseph MacDonald is the reason and you

167

know it!'

Grandfather Tolman shuffled to a chair and eased down as though every bone in his body had suddenly turned as fragile and brittle as glass. His eyes were bird-bright.

'Pat, no one could ever have twisted your arm to make you say the things you told MacDonald tonight. You did it voluntarily.'

She was on unsteady ground. He knew it as well as she did. And what he'd just said was perfectly true. They both also knew that.

He got comfortable in the chair. 'Pat, honey, let's just be man-to-man. All right? He's a fine man, honest, hardworking, in love with you, independent and—'

'But you'll interfere, Grandfather, like you always have, and that could spoil everything.'

'I? Interfere? Whatever gave you such a silly notion as that? Why, honey-child, you go right ahead and marry him and I won't even come and visit you unless you invite me.' He chuckled a nice little-old-man kind of a chuckle. 'And don't fret none about your folks. They'll come boiling in here tomorrow, and I'll talk them out of it as easy as pouring sand from an open-toed boot.'

She considered him with a sense of frustration and resignation. He would do just exactly as he'd said. He had always, in his own inimitable way, talked everyone out of anything he ever wanted to talk them out of. And he was an old man, not sickly, not frail,

168

but still, old. Whatever he'd ever done had been to shield his family. She did not have to approve of the way he did things, but she couldn't fault the reasons.

She went to the sofa, sat and shook her head. She was yielding and he hadn't even done anything yet.

He said, 'Suppose you and Mac take over the sales and promotion side of the development? But I'm not going to spend much more money up here. You two will be strictly on your own.'

'How?' she asked.

'Fifty-fifty. We'll split it right down the middle.'

'That's not fair, Grandfather. You've already put a fortune into the development.'

'Pat, I need a loss. I got to be able to show those damned Internal Revenue whelps that poor old Dave Tolman is losing his grip; that his judgement just ain't—isn't—so good any more.'

'I see. And I suppose you expect me to believe that's the only reason?'

'No. No, child; I wouldn't try to fool you. You and me, we're too much alike. The *real* reason is that I figure you and your husband'll be needing working capital for some schemes of your own, from now on. Well, according to my calculations you'd ought to net something like a million and a half dollars off the development. That ought to launch you, hadn't it?'

She sat gazing at him. 'You'll lose your shirt, Grandfather.'

'Like hell I will . . . Excuse me. No I won't. I got to have that much of a tax-write-off because that consarned factory I own in East Los Angeles went and beat its delivery schedules to the Department of Defence, and qualified for the bonus they gave—which was one and a half million dollars. Now, Pat, my capital gains will just about ruin me this year—unless I can show that much loss. Do you follow me?'

'Yes.'

Grandfather Tolman leaned back and held forth his hands, palms up. 'Pat, your folks each got big trust-funds. They couldn't go broke if they wanted to. Who's left?'

She appreciated what he was doing, as she usually did, but she had a misgiving. 'Mac may not approve, Grandfather.'

The old man dropped his hands, puckered his eyes and slyly said, 'You ever hear of any one rude enough to give back a wedding present, child? It's just not done.'

She almost smiled at him. 'You are still a fraud, Grandfather, but—'

'No buts, child.' He made a great show of struggling up to his feet, then he saw the look on her face and stood a moment before he smiled and dropped her one of his raffish winks. 'Okay, Pat, I'm a fraud. *You* know it. *I* know it. *Mac* knows it and your folks, after all these years, are beginning to wonder about it. But the blasted Internal Revenue Service doesn't know it, and so I can go to bed happy every night.' He paused as though to give her the opportunity to agree with him, but she sat silent, introspectively silent, so he said, 'Tell me flat out, child: do you really love this man?'

Whatever had seemed to be troubling her, this evidently was not it. She gave him her answer without a moment's hesitation. 'Yes. I can't give you the definite date when it happened, but I can tell you it *did* happen. He's all the things a woman wants and needs in a man, Grandfather.'

'You are right about that, child. Well; I've got to get to bed. I'm not used to staying up this late.' From over by the door he said, 'Goodnight, Pat. And quit worrying, will you. It'll make lines in your face.'

He went out into the empty, silent hallway and stepped briskly along to his own suite of rooms. They weren't exactly the rooms he'd have chosen if there'd been any choice, but since there hadn't been he was content with them.

As he shed his coat and began tugging off his tie he grinned at himself in the dressing-table mirror. 'Nothing for her to worry about. As for me interferin'—I wonder whatever gave Mac such a foolish idea? Of course I'll interfere.'

He eventually climbed into bed, punched the pillows into position and eased back. Then he laughed in the darkness after switching off the light. It had all worked out just about as he'd expected it.

Before closing his eyes he had already checked off the land development in his mind, and as he drifted off to sleep he began wondering which of the half dozen or so fresh projects he'd been thinking about lately would be the best to jump into next. After all, a frail little old man in his eighties had to make hay while the sun shone.

He slept like a baby, with a smile on his face and peace in his sturdy, old heart.

CHAPTER NINETEEN

AN EMOTIONAL TUG-OF-WAR

Grandfather Tolman did not appear for breakfast the following morning, at least while his granddaughter and MacDonald were in the dining-room, but then they ordinarily ate a bit early. Neither of them expected him to appear anyway.

Outside, as they went to Mac's car, the golden sun was sending its brilliance to precede it over the farthest peaks. In many ways this was a finer time of day than sunset.

As Patricia hesitated Mac guessed her mood.

'The world is full of promise every morning,' he said, 'and we could sit up all night debating whether mankind made it one bit better during the day.' He opened the car door for her. 'To the pond?'

She slid into the car. 'Is that still what you want, Mac?'

'You know it is,' he replied, walking round and getting in on the driver's side where he sat a moment lightly drumming on the steering-wheel. 'But we really should go up to the job and make certain everything gets started right.'

She smiled affectionately. 'I expected you to say something like that.' She gestured. 'Let's go, sitting here doesn't help any.'

He started the car, backed clear then shot across the paved area to the exit, and from there right. He seemed to Patricia to be slightly self-conscious, or perhaps it was humiliated or chagrined. She leaned to pat his hand on the wheel. 'One of us was bound to worry about leaving without even going up to make sure everyone got started this morning. If you hadn't made the suggestion I would have.'

He was relieved, or at least she felt that he was. By the time they reached the development the sun had finally popped up over that distant mountain and now there was that cathedral-light throughout the forest.

Mac unlocked the office, allowed her to

enter first, and went to swing the windows wide as well. When he turned back she was standing near the little shadowy corridor leading to the rear offices. 'Did you talk to Grandfather?' she asked. 'I mean—I know he was out there where he could watch us last night. He told me so. But did he mention the development to you last night?'

Mac shrugged. 'Mostly, he talked about corollaries; your parents, you and me, but he didn't single out the development. Why?'

'He is going to give it to us as a wedding present.'

Mac stared, then eventually twisted his face into an expression of exasperation. 'He's got at least a million bucks tied up here. That's a pretty damned ridiculous wedding present isn't it? Why couldn't he just give us well—a car, or some furniture, or maybe a set of dishes?'

'Why, love? Because he's Grandfather Tolman, that's why. And he'll have a perfectly convincing reason every time.'

'This time?'

'He owns a number of other things, Mac. There's a metal fabricating company in East Los Angeles. He told me last night it had made too much profit this past year and he had to find a loss to off-set the gain, or capital gains were going to ruin him. So, he wants to get rid of the development and call it a tax write-off. You see what I mean? It all sounds so very reasonable.'

174

'But is it?' he asked, stepping closer and leaning on a map-table. 'Did his company really come through really smelling that much like a rose?'

'I'd guess so, Mac. Grandfather Tolman isn't all that much of a sentimentalist. If things weren't as he told me, I think we'd get the car or the set of dishes. We'd get *something*, naturally, but nothing quite so valuable . . . And Mac, promise me something? Please don't pick on him.'

He leaned there eyeing her, then he threw up both hands. 'You know what I think? Grandfather Tolman's got the evil eye on all of us.'

Outside, the men were beginning to arrive. Their noise, catcalls, and rising dust churned to life beneath car wheels, signalled the arrival of a fresh day. Mac straightened up off the map-table as a foreman came stamping up over the porch and into the building. Pat discreetly faded away in the direction of the office she'd appropriated.

Of course Mac was right, Grandfather Tolman *did* have the Indian sign on everyone. But that wasn't necessarily bad. As for the wedding present, she went round behind the desk, sat down and turned to gaze out of an easterly window. No question about it, it was too much. Yet, if Grandfather Tolman actually were in the kind of tax situation where their refusal of the wedding gift would injure him, then what possible reason could they have for turning down the kind of windfall that came just once in a lifetime—and in only perhaps one out of ten thousand lifetimes at that?

She reached for the telephone, dialled the accounting firm down in the city that kept her grandfather's financial running inventory, identified herself and in the same brisk impersonal tone she had used in the past when making calls for her grandfather, asked for a quick, thumbnail summary of the manufacturing firm's financial status. The reply she got confirmed everything Grandfather Tolman had said. As she rang off she had a small, guilty twinge. But it hadn't been that she'd doubted him, it had merely been that she'd wanted to be sure, before she explained to Mac that acceptance of the wedding present wasn't simply something they should resist on general principles.

In the outer office those masculine voices were, as always, loud and gruff. There was some laughter, and Patricia detected the smell of tobacco. She liked it. She'd never cared much for the smell of cigarettes or cigars, although the former were not offensive to her, but that smell coming back to her now was of a pipe and she liked the smell of pipe-smoke. She smiled at herself. Would it have smelled half as wonderful if someone else had been making it?

She glanced at a letter needing answering

without really seeing it, and thought of something else: her own willingness, last night, to return to the lily-pad pond with him today. She wondered if they'd be able to re-create that feeling, that desire, again, now that they were in their every-day world. She felt a little wistful. She even felt mild resentment over the arrival of Grandfather Tolman, blaming him in part for the fact that they hadn't just driven out to the expressway heading back towards that rutted turn-off, instead of coming up to the development today.

Of course, that wasn't very rational. They still could have gone to the pond. If she'd been willing to run away knowing her parents would be arriving, knowing that a family crisis was approaching, then she'd have been equally willing to run away from Grandfather Tolman.

And it had been Mac's idea anyway, that they come up to the office this morning. Perhaps he'd thought over their moonlight-madness and now was repentant. That thought sunk her into gradual gloom. When he finished out front and came strolling back to loom in her doorway, she scowled up at him.

'I wish this damned development was completed!'

He leaned against the door-jamb eyeing her. 'It's near enough. But what brought that on?'

'You and your work! Being conscientious is one thing but being a fanatic is quite another.'

He sighed softly, lifted a hand to lightly

scratch his cheek, and throughout this small interval kept gauging her, probing her mood until finally he said, 'Right you are. Get your handbag and let's get out of here.' He straightened up off the door.

She lost all that annoyance in a second, then the doubts, the reservations, the excuses, came rushing in. She sat there.

He said, 'Listen, lovely lady, if there is one thing I cannot abide it's a beautiful woman who can't see beyond her work. Are you going to sit there all day?'

He was giving it right back to her. She smiled, rose and looked for her handbag. He said, 'You left it in the car. I distinctly remember that. Come along.'

The telephone shrilly interrupted as she was leaving the desk. 'Let the damned thing ring,' he growled, and reached for her arm. She looked pained, but when he had her arm she dutifully responded to his pull and went out of the office. They could hear the telephone ringing until they were down off the porch and midway to where his car was parked.

From a considerable distance she heard the deep throb of the huge yellow caterpillar D-8 cats at their prodigious labours. They could create modest lakes in a matter of days or could bulldoze a road-grade in less time. They were exorbitantly expensive to bring in and put on a job, but they could accomplish in a fifth of the time what smaller tractors would be weeks at accomplishing, at less cost. She made some mention of the cats and MacDonald told her they would be finishing up within the week, and be moving out. He smiled at her. 'Then up go the site-markers, the little pennants marking what's available—the sales campaign begins.'

She said, 'Mac, have you ever followed through on a land-development scheme before?'

'Nope. But how can I miss with you as my assistant?'

She laughed at him. 'Partner, not assistant.'

They were heading down towards the village by this time, trailing a plume of dust. Sunlight and shadow coloured their uplands world. Man, and man's creations down in the vicinity of the lodge, appeared neither very important nor very permanent. Just before they scooted past towards the expressway he said, 'You've decided we should accept the wedding present?'

She shied away from a positive statement by telling him that she had verified what her grandfather had said about needing the write-off, but his mood did not seem very affected. Finally, feeling her way, she said, 'Mac, we've either got to accept or not. If you have reservations, hadn't we better have them out?'

'It looks as if I'm marrying you for your wealth, Pat.'

She had an immediate answer: Her

Grandfather hadn't even made the offer until after he had proposed and she had accepted. But in the masculine view this evidently was nit-picking; was like suggesting he hadn't been aware of the Tolman family's wealth and that the others would want to do something extravagant for her.

Finally, as they bore along at high speed heading for the rutted turn-off, she found what she hoped would be the correct approach. 'How many hundreds of married couples inherit the family grocery store, the family farm or the dairy business? You can call that a belated dowry can't you, Mac? But if you say no to Granddad's offer of the development, I'll say no too.'

'You think I'm being unnecessarily stubborn then?'

'Yes, Mac, but whatever you decide, I'll certainly abide by it.'

He reached with one arm and swept her up close to him. He drove the last mile or two like that and while she was perfectly aware that the Highway Patrol took a dim view of one-arm-driving she could not right at that moment have cared less.

They came to the ruts and left the expressway swinging left where he had to disengage his arm to use both hands steering. He also had to slacken speed considerably.

Everything was as it had been the day before, except that the light angles were different, this being morning while the day before they'd reached this spot in the afternoon. It *did* make a difference. When they left the car as they'd done the day before, and he teased her by pointing up through the trees for her to lead the way, she found that even with familiar landmarks, the light angle made things radically different.

But she had pressed-flat grass to help, so for the first half mile she went confidently along. Then other tracks emerged, mingled, and began splitting off here and there and she had to give up.

'Deer,' he said. 'Okay, I'll lead.'

She was impressed with his unerring instinct about direction. Where she'd have sworn they should have veered one way or another, he stepped on across and pressed directly ahead.

He was right. They came to the familiar downhill slope, the little creek, and finally to the soda-spring. Later, with forest hush and coolness all around, he took her as far as the well-defined trail, then stood aside with a grin for her to lead the last few hundred yards to the lake.

Her heart had a quickened cadence for some reason, and she felt instinctively that her first glimpse of their secret and serene little pond would mean that something would shortly afterwards happen to change the tenure and the rhythm of her life for ever.

CHAPTER TWENTY

ALONE IN LOVE

He laughed at her expression as they went on down to their pond. 'You remind me of one of those people who sell aspirin on television commercials, Pat. Cheer up—the worst is yet to come.'

She smiled and shrugged, but said nothing. People being constituted differently, it seemed quite easy for him to put everything out of his mind except the immediate moment.

She was unable to do that, quite, even though she made an honest effort after his laughing rebuke, and even though she realized this was a special moment for both and she had no right to bring disharmony to it.

At least for the moment she was unable to do that.

He took her hand as they neared the pond, which was pleasant, and showed her a small green frog sitting as motionless as a tiny stone statue, watching every move they made, but when they both looked all around they saw no deer. It was too late in the morning for deer to be feeding and much too early for them to be either bedding down or heading for water.

But there were other things. She saw a bushy-tailed tree-squirrel daintily feeding on the ground, so engrossed he had no idea any two-legged things were within miles.

If he'd realized a pair of them were within easy stone's throw he'd have bypassed breakfast and raced to the top of his loftiest pine to scold.

There were two brush-rabbits, perhaps a male and female, grazing side-by-side, and somewhere up through the cool trees, blue grouse called.

She said, 'I thought we'd be alone,' and showed him the squirrel and rabbits. He nodded. 'Funny thing about people being alone in a place like this. *They* believe they are, and more hidden eyes are watching them every minute from underfoot, from overhead, from all around, than if they were in the midst of a city.' He dropped down to test the water, straightened up and said casually, 'I'm going swimming.'

She had a swim-suit under her other clothes too, but did not say so as they moved back across the grass towards the forest-fringe. He stopped abruptly, pointing, as a mother skunk with four babies, miniatures of their parent, went walking past a few yards distant. The mother saw both Pat and Mac but with a skunk's self-assurance only whisked her tail in casual warning and kept right on walking. Her four babies, a third her size, didn't even glance up. They were obediently marching in single file—shiny little black creatures with their broad white stripe and elegant, bushy tails.

The mother took them away from the tall grass to the pine-needle-poisoned clearing of a great old bull-pine, and as unafraid as she could be, decided this was the best place around for nursing her young, and proceeded to do so, her black, shoe-button eyes raised to watch as the two-legged things stood off a fair distance, observing.

Pat said, 'Just like a cat or a dog. I had no idea . . .' She smiled. 'But then I haven't known very many skunks.'

They went up to the shade.

Finally, she was able to detect all the busy sounds of this secluded glen and found them to be as numerous, almost, as the louder and more familiar sounds of the city. She mentioned this and Mac said there was no such thing as total seclusion unless one mentioned it in the sense that a member of some particular *species* came to a place where there were no other members of his particular species.

She was impressed. 'That's very good. Did you read it somewhere?'

He looked down a bit patronisingly. 'No. Any farm kid knows it. Like sex, kids raised in the country don't suddenly discover it, because it's been there all the time and they've grown up with it hardly aware it's supposed to be unusual.' He changed the subject. 'You don't happen to have brought your bathing suit along?'

She nodded.

'Okay. You go behind *that* tree and I'll go behind this one.' He had a twinkle in his eye. 'No peeking.'

She laughed although only a few days earlier she'd have blushed furiously. Also, she did as he instructed; went behind a huge old oak tree, undressed, adjusted the straps of her bathing suit and walked back out again after hanging her clothes on a low limb. He was already over there looking down towards the pool. He turned, swept her with a glance, gestured for silence and turned back. She had an odd, little tingly feeling, remnant of something from an ancient past when the hunter in the forest signalled for stillness because of a faint-heard sound.

Two big-eared does with three spotted fawns came daintily down from where the unseen watercourse fed the pond. They halted several times to look and listen, but also, they were intent on something up ahead and neglected to spy either the man in swimming trunks over across the pond standing motionless in mottled shade, or the girl in her two-piece bathing suit, tanned and sturdy and equally still, a short distance from the man.

Pat said, 'It's a shame to frighten them away,' in a low whisper. MacDonald did not answer, he was watching the deer. They turned off, not interested in drinking evidently, and kept to the far fringe of shadows over yonder.

Finally, they halted in a bare place, grouped up close and put down their heads.

Mac had his answer to the riddle. Turning and moving in Pat's direction he said, 'Salt. There's a lick over there.'

She watched the deer, backs to the pond and the people now, heads lowered, busy at whatever occupied them in half-shade, half-sunlight.

'You're beautiful,' MacDonald said.

Pat raised her eyes and turned back. He was standing ten feet away gazing at her. Now, finally, she blushed. A two-piece bathing suit left nothing to the imagination. Not that she was ashamed, but she did feel self-conscious so she said, 'If we go down and dive in it'll scare them.'

He raised his eyes to her face. They had a stillness in their depth, a sense of masculine waiting. 'And if we *don't* go swimming do you know what could happen?'

She knew, but she made no move out of her tracks as he walked on up closer. He was thick through from shoulders to chest. From there he tapered to lean thighs and powerful legs.

For a moment it was a little hard for her to breathe. When he raised his arms she stepped inside them voluntarily. Finally, too, the does across the pond detected movement and flung up their heads, watching without moving so much as an ear.

His hands across her naked shoulders, like

186

her cheek upon his bare chest, was the kind of physical contact that turned everything topsy-turvy for them both. Neither spoke and for a long while she simply lay against him feeling the surge of his heart. When he reached to tilt her face upwards she closed her eyes and kept them closed.

His lips were gentle and soft upon her. She reached higher to encircle his shoulders and press into him. When that moment was past she held him round the waist, low, and said, 'Hadn't we better go swimming?'

He agreed. 'I suppose so.' But he still held her.

Finally, he laughed and broke the spell. She felt herself being held out at arm's length. It was useless to hide the high colour, the look she knew perfectly well showed in her eyes as well as upon her lips.

'Is the pond still there?' he asked.

She smiled back. 'I don't know. I haven't looked. I just barely remember there was a pond here.'

The does were gone, having evidently stolen off during that long and bitter-sweet embrace. But of course the pond was still there.

He led her to the water's edge, out in bright sunlight. She did not resist, she wouldn't have resisted right then if he'd picked her up and thrown her in. But he simply released her and moved ahead one step, rose up and arched downward, striking the water with solid grace.

She waited for him to emerge. When he ultimately did it was two-thirds of the way across. He called back.

'There's a big old crocodile down here on the bottom.'

'A what?'

'Well, an old tree-trunk that sort of looks like an old crocodile.'

She laughed at him. 'Did you ever see a real crocodile?'

He flung water off his face, swept back his hair and faced her treading water. 'No. But I've seen Venus with golden flesh in a two-piece white bathing suit standing on the bank of a sunlighted pond in the middle of a dark forest, and I'll bet there's not another mortal man who can make *that* statement.'

She put forth a naked foot to test the water. It was chilly but not terribly so. She stepped closer and catapulted herself out ten feet before cleaving water and sinking torpedo-like heading in his direction. He watched the dive, then turned and headed off in a different direction. When she surfaced where he'd been he was not in sight.

She found the huge old sunken log and stood on it waiting for him to surface. Instead, two powerful hands gripped her ankles. She had neglected to look down. He let go, grazed her as he rose to the surface, and emerged beside her, also on the log. He flung off water and grinned. He hardly seemed like the same man she'd met a couple of weeks before. In fact, he didn't seem like the dedicated engineer of the Tolman development at all. He was more like she imagined he must have once been back in the middlewest, swimming in a farm pond. Young and strong, healthy and mischievous.

'Venus,' he said, 'if I took you out into bright sunlight would you melt?' He slid an arm round her waist. 'What can you possibly see in me, a mere mortal?'

She leaned away as though making a careful study. 'Well, on Olympus the men have no hair on their chests. For another thing, there are no ponds in forests, only marble pools lined with statues of us gods. I think I might like to be a mortal for a while.'

His grip round her waist tightened. 'Not for a while. For a very, very long time.' He swung her effortlessly.

She raised both hands, palms forward, to his chest. She said, 'Steady, lad, steady. We could drown out here like this.'

Seconds before his lips came down he said in a soulful tone, 'What a way to go!'

The log settled deeper into mud under their combined weight and grated off a stone. As it turned they fell sidewards. His arms still held her and she clung to him as well until moments after the water closed above them. Then they came loose and drifted back towards the surface.

As soon as she faced him she said, 'Mac, if you ever tell anyone you made love to your wife under water no one will believe you.'

They stroked evenly for the shore, climbed out and went back up where the shade was. Directly above them the sun had taken a position above their glade, their pool, the entire area although it had unimpeded egress only by the pool where no forest stubbornly kept it locked out.

She said they should have brought towels. He lay in the grass on his shirt looking upwards where she sat beside him. 'Ten minutes is all it takes in weather like this.' He reached to trace the roundness of her shoulder, her upper arm. 'The strangest thing is how all this happened, Pat.'

She turned. 'You didn't like me at all on first sight.'

He considered that, screwed up his face, puckered his eyes and said, 'Well, let's put it this way—I didn't like what was being done, but it only touched upon you as something being used against me.'

'That's pretty involved, lover.'

His expression cleared at once. 'Okay. Let me put it another way. On first sight I held my breath. You were beautiful. You were exquisite. You were something I'd been waiting fifteen years for. I was in love with you ten minutes after I saw you.'

'Mac MacDonald this is not true!'

He reared up, caught her and pulled her down until her back was where his had been, upon his wet shirt in the grass. 'True as anything you'll ever know, Pat,' he said, holding her motionless under him. 'I give you my word it's true.'

She had trouble breathing again. She also had some other vague difficulty. It had to do with weakness in the limbs, the joints—and the resolve.

He leaned to brush her lips with his mouth, to cradle her head in the crook of one arm. When the kiss was finished she raised both arms to him. 'You certainly didn't *act* as if you liked me, Mac.'

He pushed his face into the curve of her naked shoulder. 'How am I acting now, love of my life?'

She didn't answer. She rolled to face him. Overhead high in their pine a squirrel was outraged at such antics in his—or her—private domain.

CHAPTER TWENTY-ONE

A KIND OF RECONCILIATION

Elyse Tolman told her father-in-law in a petulant tone of voice that he'd no business in sending Pat and Mister MacDonald off, and it wasn't very nice of him to sit there at the little secluded table in the Redwood Room denying that he'd done it.

A barman brought their drinks. After the long drive up, Davey had insisted on a chilled bottle of beer so they'd gone into the bar, which was all but deserted this early afternoon time of day. Davey watched the barman pour his beer gloomily. Afterwards he said, 'Father, you made me look pretty damned ridiculous, calling Merriman and telling him to submit a bill and to forget succeeding MacDonald. That will be all over town in no time: Dave Tolman downgraded by his father.'

Grandfather Tolman didn't have a chance. Elyse, after several swallows of her gin and coke, was at him again. 'Doctor Severns said never again; he was so angry that you'd got out of bed and had driven up here all alone. He said he wasn't going to remain as your personal physician any more.'

Davey finished the beer and signalled for another. It may not have made him feel much cooler but it certainly made him feel much less sorry for himself. 'Just for the hell of it,' he said, looking steadily at his father, 'will you explain why you had to throw your only granddaughter—and our only child—to this, this construction engineer, instead of some decent stockbroker or banker or investment securities dealer—at least?'

Grandfather Tolman sipped gin and tonic,

let the successive waves of bitterness wash over him, and when his opportunity came he detonated both barrels. 'You two don't even know Joe MacDonald. He's exactly what your precious daughter needs. A red-blooded, two-fisted man with hair on his chest, both feet on the ground, and tough.' Grandfather Tolman glared. He wasn't the pitiful, little, old, frail Grandfather Tolman now, because obviously that wasn't the appropriate role.

'And I didn't *send* them off, they went without me even knowing it.'

'Well, you must get them back right away,' pouted Elyse.

'How in hell can I?' the old man exclaimed. 'I have no idea where they went. Anyway— your daughter is twenty-three years—'

'My daughter,' burst out irate Elyse, 'is twenty-two years of age.'

'Until when?' snapped the old man. 'Until next month. Ellie, you're a confounded nit-picker.'

'A—what? Davey, did you hear what your father just said to me?'

Davey had his second beer. He looked sternly at his father. 'It appears to me you can be a little more courteous,' he pronounced.

Grandfather Tolman flared up, struggled briefly, then nodded. 'Sorry, Ellie. Anyway, a nit-picker isn't anything terrible. A nit's just a baby louse. You sometimes find folks who pick the baby lice and overlook the grown, sassy-fat ones.'

'Of all the crude, disgusting talk I ever heard,' bleated Elyse. 'And Grandfather Tolman you know I don't like to be called Ellie.'

'Elyse,' said the old man, still giving ground, but assuaging his chagrin with a sip now and then. 'Look, Elyse, the girl's well past the age of consent. It isn't *healthy*, you two tryin' to keep her a kid so long. Now, with MacDonald, she's going to become a real woman overnight—ah, excuse me—a real woman in no time at all. *That's* blamed important, don't you see that? And Elyse—there's one more thing,' Old Tolman paused to include his son in this by raking a narrowed glance over Davey too. 'They're on their own. At least they will be in a couple of days, as soon as my lawyers down in L.A. finish drawing up the papers and preparing the deeds for signatures and transfers and recordings.'

Davey's second beer was gone. He wavered between trying to catch the barman's eye, and permitting his own eye to be captured by his father's stare. He gave up on the bartender. 'What deeds are you talking about, Father?'

'I give 'em the development.'

'Why aren't you more careful with your grammar, Father? You *gave* them the deeds to . . . *You what*?'

'I *gave* them the damned development, lock, stock, and barrel. Sort of a wedding present.'

Davey gazed helplessly over at his wife, who had the attention of the barman, finally, and was gesturing for a refill for herself and her husband, but none for Grandfather Tolman.

Davey drifted his glance back to his father. 'You've done it again, you realize.'

The old man nodded. 'Yes, I know. But you couldn't have brought it off anyway, gettin' control because I'm old and sick and maybe incompetent. Davey, I didn't want to fight you. It makes for bad feeling between father and son.'

'So you gave it to Patricia and this man.'

'Well, there was another reason. Two other reasons in fact. I need a capital loss this year, for one thing, and they'll need a slight assist to start out on.'

The barman brought another beer for Davey, another iced highball for Elyse, and departed. No one heeded him. Davey loosened where he sat, dropped his glance to the collar of foam on his fresh beer and sighed as he reached.

'You know,' he said conversationally to his father, 'you've stuck your damned neck out a mile.'

Elyse looked reproachfully across the table. 'Davey, don't swear.'

Grandfather Tolman's narrowed eyes twinkled. 'He always does when he's getting high. In fact, Elyse, that's the only time my son really acts very much like a man.'

Davey was not distracted. 'Suppose she marries this MacDonald. Suppose they fight like cat and dog and within a year get a divorce. You know what they are going to think of you, Dad, for manoeuvring them into this mess?'

Grandfather Tolman leaned back smiling. 'Sure, son, I know. Now let *me* tell you something. All my life I've been judging people and gambling on my judgements. Not on companies or machinery or markets—on *people*. There isn't a gawddamned company on this earth that ain't *people*. You want to know my secret, Dave? I just told it to you. Forget the markets, the machines, the politics, and make your decisions based on people. I've missed a few. When I was a young man I lost half a million dollars, on one bad judgement, once. But I never did that again and I'm not gambling now.'

'They won't fight, eh?'

'Well sure they'll fight, dammit. We're fightin' right now, aren't we? But that don't mean I'm goin' to disinherit you, does it? You and Ellie squawk at each other every now and then like a pair of turkey-buzzards, but you been married a long time, haven't you? Hell's bells, son, you *got* to have squabbles, don't you? Look, you two were all set to do somethin' pretty damagin' to me, weren't you, and I'm the one person on this damned globe who's put you where you are. But that's all

196

finished and we're sitting here having a drink, aren't we? And Pat's got my disposition, so she'll flare up at MacDonald now and then.' Grandfather Tolman leaned to emphasize his next words. 'But take my word for it, if she flares up too much, she'll get took across a big man's knee, and that's exactly what she's goin' to need for a few years, until she's got some kids and some decent responsibilities the kind that make *intelligent* women mature.' For several seconds Grandfather Tolman still leaned, looking as though he dared someone to refute or challenge him. No one did so he gradually turned and made a scowlingly peremptory gesture towards the barman.

Davey pushed away his empty beer glass, shoved his long legs out and glanced about the large, blessedly cool empty room as though he had nothing at all on his mind. He was perspiring and rumpled, and after that long drive and the nagging bleating of his wife, he seemed either quite at peace, or resigned.

Elyse declined a refill when the barman brought Grandfather Tolman his second gin and tonic. Davey looked up with a droll smile and called for a gin and tonic also. The barman started away before Elyse said, scowling darkly, 'David, you've had enough. Besides, if you mix those things in your stomach you'll get a headache. You always do.'

Davey gazed at his wife. 'Who's damned belly is it, anyway?'

'*David Tolman!*' Elyse gasped. 'You are being rude!'

When the glasses came Grandfather Tolman eyed his son. 'Want a nickel's worth of advice, Dave?'

'No, but I'll get it anyway. So shoot.'

'*Buy in with MacDonald.* Put up half the money and get him to find another section of land, then the three of you develop and peddle it in sites. Let Pat do the promotional and secretarial work. Dave, you can't make money. You've never had the knack. But a shrewd man with some operating capital—like I said a minute ago—makes his judgements, and takes his gamble on *people*. My opinion is that Pat and Mac will make a damned fine team. After half a century of perfecting my system, I know exactly what I'm talking about.'

David Tolman sat all relaxed and pleasant with the untouched but iced glass in his hand, and lifted his eyes towards his wife across the table. He didn't say anything, he just looked.

Grandfather Tolman raised his wrist, stared, then pushed away his drink and rose. 'I darned near forgot. I have to do some work upstairs in my room. See you two in an hour or two. By the way, when you're tanked up in the bar, why not go upstairs and take a nap in Pat's room. Then you'll be fresh when she comes in?'

He didn't wait for an answer, but turned and went briskly out of the Redwood Room. The 'work' he had to do upstairs was take a nap. He tried to take one every afternoon. If he didn't, he invariably got drowsy at the dinner-table, and shortly afterwards, when people ordinarily had their best conversations. It was, Grandfather Tolman knew full well, part of the degenerative process of getting old, but the nap got around it very handily. He knew a dozen ways of getting around these degenerative processes and used every one of them.

Elyse sighed, considered the huge diamond solitaire she wore, and said, 'You're not going to take his advice, are you, Davey?'

'Why shouldn't I—Ellie?'

Her blue eyes lifted and went to her husband with a hard chill. 'Are you trying to pick a fight by calling me that, Davey?'

He nodded. 'Yes. I think so. You know how old I am?'

'Certainly. What a ridiculous thing to ask your own wife!'

'Yeah? Then how come you still call me Davey?'

The blue eyes wavered. 'I see,' Elyse said coldly. 'You are determined to be disagreeable.'

'Nothing of the kind, Ellie. I love you. I still do. Isn't that odd? Do you remember who manoeuvred us into marriage?'

She didn't move for a while, but eventually her lips softened, her eyes slid to the beaded glass near at hand Grandfather Tolman had abandoned untouched, and she nodded. 'Yes, I remember—David.'

He grinned. 'Elyse.'

'Oh. I suppose Ellie's all right. It just sounds so—low-class, though.'

They smiled at one another. She said, 'Shouldn't we go up and shower and take a nap? It was a long drive, and he was right, we'll want to look fresh when Patricia comes in.'

'Sure. About him deeding the development over to them . . .'

'It was really very sweet of him, David.'

'And that other idea: Us putting up half the money and getting into the land-development business with them?'

'Uh . . . well, he didn't include me in that, David, so I guess the decision will have to be yours.'

He placed both hands upon the edge of the table and pushed himself upright. He wasn't drunk but he would have been if he'd downed that untouched glass he left behind. Moreover, Elyse was quite correct; mixing all that beer with gin and tonic was like inhaling rat poison. He'd have survived, but there would _he_ moments he was neither sure he would, nor sure he'd care to.

The lodge was wonderfully cool and quiet as they left the Redwood Room bound across the lobby towards the stairway. By the time they reached the upstairs landing David was already beginning to yawn. Farther along, in his own rooms, Grandfather Tolman was dead to the world and happily snoring. Outside, the afternoon waned steadily, each hour inexorably following the preceding one, heading towards evening.

CHAPTER TWENTY-TWO

THE UNDERSTANDING

There was usually a good bit of traffic over the Grapevine, even during winter when the road at high elevations was icy and very dangerous, but in summertime with the only coolness being at the crest, and also because the Grapevine was one of the major arterial expressways leading out of Los Angeles at this especially busy time of the holiday season, it could he counted upon to be crowded even though it had four lanes for outgoing traffic, separated by a metal divider-strip, from another four lanes for incoming traffic. If there was any gratification in this fact, the *in*coming traffic, from over on the Bakersfield side of the Coast Range Mountains was invariably lighter than the traffic pouring out of Los Angeles.

As Mac said, with an explanatory gesture towards the distant, ominously black cloud above the Los Angeles area, anyone who voluntarily lived in that filthy, unhealthy atmosphere had to be insane, and evidently there weren't many at that, judging by the four-wheeled exodus over in the outgoing lanes.

It was much easier to get down to Bakersfield, and back to Crestline again, than it was to try to reach Los Angeles. Also, Bakersfield was closer, and although it had not been the case at one time, it now was: anything to be found in the larger city could also be found in the smaller one. Or, put another way, the ring on Patricia's finger, like the wedding licence in MacDonald's pocket, was every bit as elegant and official although procured in Bakersfield as either would have been if procured in Los Angeles.

And Pat was just as radiant too, as she leaned with her head on MacDonald's shoulder half-hypnotised by the headlamps of the car as Mac headed steadily towards Crestline Village. Once, she spoke.

'Do you suppose someone had the sense to lock the office?'

He smiled. 'I wouldn't bet on it, unless of course your grandfather went up there.'

She sighed, snuggled closer and was content with that. Or perhaps she'd only been talking to break the long silence that had preceded her remark. After another mile or so she said, 'Do you suppose my parents arrived all right?'

'They will have arrived,' he concurred,

omitting those last two words. 'By now the fur should have been flying long enough for most of it to settle. If it's any consolation by the time we get up there maybe each side will have worn the other side down a bit.'

She pressed closer. 'Two against the many.'

He considered that. 'I doubt if your grandfather will be troublesome, but I flinch at the tears your mother will shed at what we've done. I'm sure she can't possibly approve of construction engineers as sons-in-law.'

'She's not marrying one, *I* am, and *I* approve of them.'

He slid an arm round her waist. 'It's got to be the altitude. Two weeks ago we were ready to bring in the troops.' He looked at her. 'I'll tell you what I was afraid of. You. just you.'

'Still?' she asked.

They exchanged a look and he made no reply as the turn-off loomed ahead. Crestline was over a slight rise and down the off-ramp, not far, but for a moment or two out of sight.

'I just wonder,' he said, 'how far you will go in what lies ahead of us, down there.'

She straightened beside him. 'What do you mean—how far I'll go? Before you answer I'll tell you: Just as far as I can—then a little farther.'

He nodded. 'I think I knew it, love. Well, there's the lodge.'

Every window glowed orange and out front, above the verandah roof, was the yellow-lighted sign. The cars were lined up, as usual, outside the post-and-rider fence; on the verandah people moved, cigarette-tips glowed. MacDonald eased around to his parking place, switched off the car and held to the wheel for a moment, as though dredging up his defences, or as though perhaps blaming himself for causing all this.

Patricia reached in front of him, swung his door open and said, 'March!' She smiled as he turned towards her, rose a little to meet his lips, and afterwards got out on her side of the car, went round to him with the beautiful diamond ring flashing, felt for his hand and when he'd perhaps have gone round back, she tugged him towards the front promenade leading to the steps and on up to the porch.

People were out there, mostly men who worked at the development, a few with wives. Most of the single, younger men were across the road at the tavern, which may have been just as well. There were some elaborately casual greetings exchanged, then Mac held the door and Patricia passed through into the lighted lobby.

The manager saw them and hastened over, saw the cameo brooch and beamed at Patricia, then at Mac. 'She liked it, eh?'

Mac looked mildly disgusted. He saw Pat's gaze rise to his face. 'I took Frank's wife to Bakersfield to help me select something you'd like,' he said. 'The brooch was really her idea.'

204

Aside, to the lodge manager, he growled. 'Big-mouth.' Then he'd have led Patricia away but the manager stopped them.

'Some folks waiting in the dining-room for you.' He led and they dutifully followed.

It was her parents, and Grandfather Tolman, sitting at a somewhat isolated table, having dinner. Mac dropped his lips to Pat's ear and said, 'The lion is lying down with the lambs.'

She squeezed his fingers as they approached the table, were seen as the manager winked and turned to walk off.

It was an awkward moment, with the men standing, greeting one another, and with Elyse sitting, staring at her daughter's diamond engagement ring. She gulped. MacDonald was sure she was going to embarrass everyone by bursting into tears, but she fooled him. She looked at him very soberly, almost lugubriously, then held up her hand. It was like a signal. Everyone sat, and a waiter came with two menus. MacDonald, the eater of big-suppers, ordered a salad and some tea. Pat looked sympathetically at him and ordered the same. Then, because no one else seemed willing to do so, she took the initiative, showed them her ring, and said, 'We got the wedding licence down in Bakersfield late this afternoon, otherwise we'd have been back sooner. I'm sorry, Mother—Dad, if I caused you to worry.'

Grandfather Tolman, usually ready with words, was quiet, but his expression hinted that he wasn't really surprised at any of this, and that perhaps he'd known all along it would happen.

His son, freshly shaved and dressed and looking as though he hadn't had a hectic day at all, said to MacDonald: 'Is it Mac, or do we call you Joe?'

'Mac. Although I answer to both. And I echo Pat's words about being sorry if we caused you worry.'

David's lips lifted slightly, his eyes considered MacDonald. 'The time was well spent—for us at any rate.'

It perhaps appeared to Grandfather Tolman that the conversation was floundering, which it was, because he suddenly brought forth a stiff, folded paper from an inside pocket and proceeded to unfold it as he explained that he hadn't wanted to bring this up until the entire family was on hand, but as a matter of fact he had only recently located another parcel of land, slightly larger this time, a full six hundred and forty acres, a little closer to the city but still on the Grapevine, in fact bordering the road itself this time, which from the re-sale standpoint was very desirable.

He would have put the map he'd been unfolding over the tabletop, dishes and all, but the waiter arrived with two salads and pre-empted the space. Afterwards his son, with a determined scowl said, 'Wait a minute. Let's understand each other. Are you going to propose that Mac supervises this new development?'

The old man considered his son's hard look. He was not exactly patronising in the face of this obvious dissent, but he seemed very confident of himself. 'Something like that, Dave. You got objections?'

'Just one. I thought we agreed earlier, in the bar, that if I could get Mac interested in taking on another development, I would share in it, not you.'

Grandfather Tolman smiled and started to make a little deprecating gesture. Then he saw the way Elyse was gazing at him. At the way his granddaughter was also looking at him, and finally, the sardonic, amused expression up around MacDonald's eyes. What Grandfather Tolman saw, and what Mac put into words, was determined opposition.

'You aren't going to win this one,' said Mac. 'It looks to me, Mister Tolman, as though you've pushed these people just about as far as they'll be pushed.'

The old man's attitude underwent an immediate change. 'Pushed? I'm not pushing anyone. It's just that a few weeks back when I saw how well this present undertaking was panning out, I commenced—on the sly sort of—looking around for another parcel of land, and—'

'Do you want to sell it?' asked David.

The old man's brows dropped low. 'Sell it? Davey, I practically stole it. It'll net twice what this present development will make. Of course I don't want to sell it.'

Dave turned to MacDonald. He explained what he'd discussed earlier with his father, a mutual participation partnership on a new development with Mac supervising, and Patricia managing promotion and sales. With a hard look at the older man, his father, Dave said, 'Just the three of us.'

Patricia reached below the table, found MacDonald's hand and squeezed it, hard, indicating that she favoured her father's proposal.

Mac, still with his sardonic small smile, faced Grandfather Tolman. 'Looks like the tribe has closed ranks against you.'

The old man sat, still with his map in both hands, looking from one to the other. Again his mood underwent a change. Now, he was the pitiful little old man again, frail and wheedling and faltering.

'My own family,' he quavered. 'Even if I didn't have the business savvy. Even if I couldn't bankroll this new development, would you cut your old grandpappy out? A man my age only has a few pleasures left. And who knows, I could go just like that.' He snapped his fingers. 'You wouldn't want it on your conscience that my last days were made sorrowful, would you?'

Mac selected a fork, considered his untouched salad and went to work on it. Beside him, Patricia did the same. Pat's father signalled for a waiter and ordered a glass of beer. Elyse was studying the other people in the dining room.

Grandfather Tolman sat perfectly still taking this all in, then he folded his map, stuffed it back into a pocket and rose from the table and without another word turned and went out of the dining-room, slumped and discouraged. At least he managed to project that impression. Mac turned to watch him go. When he turned back he was smiling softly. So were the others. Elyse said, 'It's so hard not feeling sorry for him.'

Her husband wagged his head ruefully. 'He'll never change. Never.'

The conversation turned to other things and the meal was pleasant and easy for those remaining at the table. Elyse and Pat discussed the forthcoming wedding, leaving Mac and Dave out of it. When the meal was finished Pat and her mother, still enthused with plans, departed in the direction of the upstairs rooms while Mac and Pat's father went to the bar for one more drink.

Later, Pat's father said he was going upstairs to shower and retire early. He also said, 'Will you seriously consider the partnership proposal?'

Mac nodded. 'Nothing to consider, really. If I'm boss and Pat's manager, it's a deal.' He smiled and extended his hand, and after the older man had left, he bought another drink, lit his pipe and sat for a while making some of the adjustments he would have to face as a husband, as a part of the Tolman investment syndicate, and as an engineer with wider horizons opening on all sides.

Finally, he strolled outside to the front verandah, nearly deserted now, to finish his smoke. Across the road tavern-lights glowed and a sound of distant music came from that direction. He wondered, since he had a good crew already working for him, and since it was so difficult getting that kind of a crew together in the first place, if it wouldn't be possible to move men and equipment on to the new development as he phased them out of the old one.

From the near shadows a bird-like old voice said, 'Well, no one ever wins them all, do they?'

Mac continued to smoke. He didn't even turn to look over where Grandfather Tolman was sitting in gloom as he said, 'You didn't lose and you know it.'

'What do you mean? You saw them cut me out.'

Mac smiled and finally turned his head. 'You knew they'd buck you. If you'd really wanted *them* out and *you* in, you'd never have

210

chosen that particular moment to bring up this new development. Mister Tolman, you manoeuvred them into doing just exactly what they did. You *wanted* it just like it worked out.'

'You're sure of that, are you?'

'I'm sure.'

The old man let go a ragged sigh. 'Everybody picks on me because I'm old.'

Mac laughed aloud, then lowered his pipe and exchanged a long look with Grandfather Tolman, then the old man permitted himself a wispy grin and shrugged. 'Okay. You're right. But I'm not so sure I like havin' a young buck in the tribe who sees through me like you do.' He got up. 'I'm goin' to bed. Goodnight, Mac. And incidentally—I was only joshin'. I'm right proud to have you in the family.' He extended a hand. They shook, then, as the old man went towards the yonder doorway Mac watched him, and when the old man passed from sight Mac laughed again, shook his head wryly, and went back to puffing on his pipe.

We hope you have enjoyed this Large Print book. Other Chivers Press or G.K. Hall & Co. Large Print books are available at your library or directly from the publishers.

For more information about current and forthcoming titles, please call or write, without obligation, to:

Chivers Press Limited
Windsor Bridge Road
Bath BA2 3AX
England
Tel. (01225) 335336

OR

G.K. Hall & Co.
P.O. Box 159
Thorndike, Maine 04986
USA
Tel. (800) 223-2336

All our Large Print titles are designed for easy reading, and all our books are made to last.